MW00946411

The Journeys of Gershom and Jasmine

Jessica Fortenberry

Second Edition published in 2021
Printed in the United States of America

Dedication:

To my husband Bill—

who never gave up his vision of seeing my book in print

To my son William—

who is a daily inspiration to me with his tender heart

To the Author of everything, my adopted Father, God—

Who gave me the wherewithal and creativity

to write in the first place

Contents

Prologue—Newman's Corner, NY
Four Years Ago

"Say hello to your new family, Gershom."

Clarice pushed eight-year-old Gershom toward the red brick house where a happy couple stood on the porch. Gershom's "new mom" knelt down and opened her arms.

"They know I'm not a puppy, right?" Gershom asked his social worker. He eyed the scene before him, trying to decide if he should be as excited as his foster mom was. Clarice didn't answer him, so he sighed, picked up the black trash bag full of his belongings, and with one last backward glance, trudged up the sidewalk.

As the sound of Clarice's jeep faded down the street, Gershom glanced around the inside of his new home. His eyes slowly widened, and his bag slipped from his grip. The first thing he noticed was freshly baked cookies. He hadn't smelled that chocolaty goodness since…maybe ever. A wet nose nudged his hand, and he knelt down to hug the golden retriever.

Mr. Peters came over to Gershom. "Would you like to see your room?" he asked.

Gershom stood and picked up his bag. "Show me the way," he said, already getting his hopes up that he found his forever family.

Two weeks later, the question was still bugging Gershom: what would it take to become adopted? Mr. Peters was the perfect father, teaching Gershom to ride a bike and the best way to hold a football to get a flawless spiral, even though he really wasn't into football. Mrs. Peters was the perfect mother, fixing a full home-cooked meal every single night—but not making him eat the green beans—and always helping him with his homework.

When Gershom's monthly visitation with his six-year-old sister finally rolled around, he was beyond excited to see her. After their usual hugs and kisses, Gershom couldn't hold it in any longer. Bouncing at their designated table in the Office of Children and Family Services, Gershom blurted out, "Jazzie, I love my new home! The family is amazing! We always—what's the matter, Jazzie?" Gershom froze mid-sentence.

Jasmine sat there listening with tears streaming down her face. "Do they have room for one more?" she whispered.

Gershom opened his mouth to speak, only to shut it again. He was having the time of his life— literally, since this was the best foster home he could remember—and his sister was in misery. They'd both had placements that didn't work out right away, but her tears concerned him. More than that, though, they made him mad.

On his way home that evening, he asked his social worker about it. "Miss Clarice," he began from the backseat, careful to keep his voice polite.

She hummed in response, not quite paying attention to him.

"My sister doesn't like her family. I'm worried about her. And the Peters are great, and they have another empty room. Can you please—"

Clarice cut Gershom off. "No, Gershom. Jasmine is fine. She's just being dramatic. Besides, you two are stuck in foster care forever. May as well get used to it."

Gershom sat there, shocked. "Why are we stuck?" he demanded, tears threatening.

Clarice waved a hand in the air. "When your mother left you and Jasmine at that church, she didn't sign papers saying you could be adopted. She just left. And no judge will approve an adoption without the birth mother signing away her rights first." She glanced in the rearview mirror at Gershom to make sure he understood. His face was all scrunched up, so she added, "Just get it out of your head that you'll be adopted one day, because we'd have to find your mom and have her sign stuff, and she ain't signing nothing."

Clarice smacked the steering wheel and cursed under her breath before checking the rearview again.

Gershom sat still, his mind spinning in a hundred different directions.

Before Gershom could do anything about finding his mother, the police banged down the door to the Peters' house. They had arrest warrants for both adults. Gershom hid in his room until a police officer did a last sweep of the house and found him, angrily sobbing into his pillow.

"Come on, buddy. Let's find you a home where the adults aren't into illegal activities." The officer ushered Gershom outside, where he called Clarice. As Gershom waited, he seethed. *I guess I don't need to find my mother and have her sign over her rights. Miss Clarice is right—I am NEVER getting adopted, but not because of any ol' paper that isn't signed. I'm not gonna let any family trick me like this again.*

1 — Gershom's Daring Plan
First Friday in May

My eyes popped open. The cobwebs hung down from the ceiling, reaching toward me like witches' fingers. I grimaced and shook my head. Standing on my bed wouldn't help much to clean them away, since my mattress sat just six inches from the floor. I grabbed a clean shirt out of my trash bag—what passed as luggage for most foster kids—and stuffed my pajamas down the inside of the bag.

"Mother" was in the kitchen doing something. The acrid smell of burnt bacon had woken me up, and I heard cabinet doors and pots and pans banging, mingling with the occasional curse word. I stepped over to my foster brother's mattress and nudged him awake with my foot.

"Dude," Justin groaned.

I leaned down and warned, "Abigale is in the kitchen, cooking. Something must be wrong—get up!"

Justin rolled over toward the wall. "Leave me alone. I'm sick today."

Whatever. Justin may not care, but I wasn't going to loiter in the bedroom until Marcus or Abigale came in to investigate what was taking us so long.

After a quick stop in the bathroom where I noticed my short black curls were getting longer than I liked them—I'd have to ask Miss Hannah to schedule me another hair cut soon. Even though I couldn't stand it when someone else touched my hair, long curls annoyed me even more—I peeked around the corner to see if "Father" was already at the table. It was Friday, and Marcus didn't usually go to work on Fridays because he said the weekend always felt like it should start a day early. Strangely, he was nowhere in sight.

"Gershom! Breakfast! Mother fixed you bacon this morning!" Abigale's shrill voice made me wince. *One of these days*...but I let the thought trail off. Pasting on a fake smile, I rounded the corner and sat down at the table. I winced again when Abigale dropped a plate in front of me. She never made breakfast.

She was never even awake at this hour to make breakfast. And where was Marcus? This morning wasn't making any sense.

"Thank you for the—bacon. Where is Mar—Father?" I hated calling Marcus and Abigale "Mother" and "Father," but I had learned the hard way that those were the only acceptable names for the adults in this house.

Abigale paused, her hand halfway to brush her frizzy hair out of her face. Her eyes darted to the clock, then the door. "He, uh, had an errand to run. Now eat your food before I think you're being ungrateful!" With that, she stomped out of the cramped kitchen and slammed her bedroom door. A minute later, I heard her shouting, presumably on the phone with Marcus. I quickly dumped my burnt offering out the back door. Maybe one of the alley cats would appreciate the free breakfast.

I tiptoed to the front door, hoping to leave before Abigale got off the phone. No such luck.

She flung open her bedroom door and yelled through the house, "After school today you're both going back to that home! The state just don't pay us enough to keep your sorry lot." She slammed her door shut again and resumed yelling at Marcus.

I closed my eyes against the thought, frozen halfway out the door. Sent back? Already? Not that I was complaining much. As far as foster parents went, Marcus and Abigale must look great on paper, but they sure didn't treat their kids right.

The yelling from their bedroom stopped, and I eased the door shut behind me. I patted my jacket pocket just to make sure. I usually brushed my teeth in the bathroom before school, and I always kept my toothbrush in my jacket pocket. I was proud to say I've been able to keep this particular toothbrush for almost five months. No foster kid ever kept their toothbrush that long if they bounced around as much as I did; I had learned the trick was to keep it with me all the time, so when Miss Hannah, my current social worker from the Office of Children and Family Services (or OCFS for short) showed up with no warning, I was ready to go.

From my front step, I looked left. At the corner of the street three houses down stood a handful of other kids, waiting for the bus. I looked right. Across the street and two houses down that way lived another foster family who had my sister. Most of the time we lived in the same school district, but this time we were lucky enough to be on the same street. I glanced back at the bus stop and saw that Jasmine wasn't there yet, so I made a split decision and turned right.

This was ridiculous, being shuttled from one horrid, rat-infested hole to the next with no warning. Last week I had overheard our social worker talking to her manager at OCFS about our mother—our birth mother—and that she still lived in Auburn. Auburn was just a couple towns up from Newman's Corner, so it should be just a hop-skip-and-jump to there. Determined, I jogged over to my sister's house.

This weekend, Jasmine and I were going to find our birth mother. A couple years ago, I had decided we didn't need her to sign her rights away, after all. But if she would simply say that we could both move in with her…One way or another, I was getting a decent-enough home where Jaz and I could both stay together, even if we were the ones ending up doing all the work.

"Hey Gersh. Ready for school today?" Jasmine closed her front door right as I got to the porch steps. She didn't look anything like I looked at age ten. She looked…happy. Bouncy. Maybe even a little carefree. I hated to burst her bubble of happiness, but important things were going to happen today.

"Jaz, we're not going to school today. Do you have your toothbrush?" I glanced around to make sure nobody was close enough to hear me.

Jasmine took a step back. "What do you mean, not going to school? Miss Hannah said it's important not to cut. We don't want to end up in the gutter someday!" She shook her head and tried to brush past me, but I grabbed her arm.

"I know school is important, but it's just for today. We're going to find our mother—our birth mother. She lives in Auburn, and if we catch the next bus, we can be there by lunch time, easy. I heard Miss Hannah talking about it."

Even as I said it, I realized what an undertaking this would be. What if we got there and our mother still didn't want us? Auburn wasn't as small of a town as Newman's Corner; how would we find her? It wasn't like we could ask the police. They would just ship us right back here.

Jasmine broke into my thoughts. "You're crazy! Running away is as bad as cutting school! Besides, the Whitmans are lovely people. They even let me stay up late on Fridays."

I shook my head. "I'm not running away. Marcus and Abigale are sending me back today." I thought for a second and smiled at my sister. "Actually, you will be the one running away."

A little pout formed on Jasmine's mouth. "So why can't we go tomorrow? Why does it have to be now?"

"I'll be back at the home tomorrow. I won't be able to come get you." I gave her my best *please* face and tacked on one more argument. "Anyways, we're almost teenagers. We'll be eleven and thirteen this summer. That's old enough to find our mother and ask why we are here and not with her. We're old enough to know the truth. Don't you want to know the truth, Jaz?"

Tears welled up in her eyes, and I knew I had her. Emotional pleas always worked on Jasmine, even though I didn't understand them. She threw her arms around me and whispered in my ear, "You're my brother; I can't let you go off alone. Then where would I be?"

I patted her back and pulled away. "Good. Now how about that toothbrush?" I had taught her the trick of keeping her toothbrush in her jacket. She had said she wanted to leave one in her bathroom at the Whitman's, so I made her get two—never can be too careful, I always said.

She pulled it out of her pocket and said, "Check! Oh! Do you have any money?"

"Not much, but it will get us to Auburn. Do you have any?"

"Nope. Where did you get money from? Please tell me you didn't steal it, because that is definitely worse than running away."

I felt for the rip in my jacket pocket and pulled out my envelope of cash. Last time I checked, there was $50.56 in it. A quick peek assured me that none of the coins were missing.

"I didn't steal it!" Goodness, what did she take me for? "Twenty is from my birthday four years ago—remember Miss Hannah said an aunt or somebody felt bad and sent a card for me?" I paused to consider this. Four years ago, our social worker retired from the business, and a month later, I got this money. I thought for sure if an aunt had really sent it, we'd have heard about her since, but could Clarice really have left me money? I shook my head, dislodging the thought.

"And then every Saturday for the past three weeks, I've mowed the lawn on the corner house. They paid me ten bucks each time. I was supposed to mow their lawn again tomorrow, but now that's not gonna happen." The fifty-six cents I had had for ages. When I first came into foster care when I was three-and-a-half, they said that I had two quarters and six pennies in my pocket, and since it was such a small amount, the social workers decided to let me keep it. How generous of them.

A loud honk startled us. I thrust my money back in my pocket, whirled around, and then sighed. It was just the bus. The door was open, and the driver stared out at us.

"Any day now!"

Our bus driver was in a bad mood every day, but Fridays were worse. I wondered if he felt like the weekend started a day early, too. I waved my hand at the bus and said in my important voice,

"Go on. My sister doesn't feel well today."

The driver sneered at me and closed the door, probably muttering something about stupid foster kids under his breath. Whatever. We had things to do and places to go, and we couldn't let a nasty school bus driver deter us.

When the bus drove out of sight, an idea popped into my head. I took Jasmine's hand, and we started walking down the sidewalk toward OCFS. I knew how we would find our mother.

2 — Jasmine and the Search

Gershom grabs my hand, and we start walking. I have to run to keep up because my legs are two years shorter than his.

"Gersh, where are we going? I thought the bus station was the other way."

Gershom nods his head. "It is. We're not going there first. We have to know where exactly it is we're going. Auburn's too big to just wander around, so we're going to find our mother's address in our file at OCFS. We'll walk in and ask to be seen to Miss Hannah's office. Then you can create a distraction so I can look up our file. Then we'll sneak out. In and out in five minutes. It's a foolproof plan."

Stealing files doesn't sound any better than running away, but I feel committed. I decide that since it is our information, we're not really stealing anything. When we get to the intersection, we turn left, then right, then right again. After a few minutes, I'm totally lost, until finally we turn a corner and there's the big brick building, a sign proclaiming "Office of Children and Family Services" hanging slightly lopsided over the door on the far right. I don't see Miss Hannah's car in the lot, so maybe I won't have to make a distraction. Maybe this will be easy.

The bell over the door jingles as we go inside. I cringe, remembering how many times I'd sat in this lobby, waiting for a new placement.

The lady behind the window slides the pane open and asks politely, "What can I do for you children?"

We walk up to the counter and Gershom squeezes my hand. I think that means for me to be quiet. He can be so bossy sometimes, even without saying a word.

"We would like to be shown to Miss Hannah's office, please."

I'm proud of him for remembering to say please. Maybe this nice lady with big red hair will let us back there. Gershom squeezes my hand again, and I smile. I even show my teeth. I hate showing my teeth because I know I need braces. The Whitmans finally got permission to take me to the orthodontist, and I sure hope we'll be back from Auburn before my appointment next Tuesday.

The lady smiles back at me and the door buzzes. Gershom pushes me through and nods at the lady.

“Thank you. We know the way.”

The lady nods and follows us anyway. I raise my eyebrows at Gershom. What are we going to do now?

“Sit,” the receptionist says. She pulls her cell phone out and types for a few seconds, then taps the door frame. “Miss Hannah is two minutes away. Think you can behave yourselves that long?”

Gershom plops into one of the overstuffed chairs, and I ease myself into the other one.

“Sure, no problem,” Gershom says. He folds his arms and scoots down into his chair, getting comfortable.

The receptionist nods at me and leaves. Her footsteps echo down the hallway, and we hear the click of her door.

Gershom jumps up. “You stand guard while I look in the filing cabinet.” He slides open the bottom drawer.

“Why don’t you start at the top?” I ask. Seems only reasonable to me to start at the beginning.

“Our last name starts with ‘Y’. That’s at the end of the alphabet, so our file should be at the bottom. Let me know if the receptionist comes back or when Miss Hannah gets here.”

Glancing back to watch Gershom flip through files, my heart feels like someone reached in there and squeezed it. He’s such a nice boy, maybe a little bossy, but he always has time to explain things to me, even when we’re in a hurry. I roll my eyes at all the behavioral tests he had when he was younger. They said he's on a spectrum of something, but he seems perfectly normal to me.

"Ah-ha!"

I turn around and see Gershom standing at the desk with a file open in front of him.

"Is that ours?" I ask. I take one last look down the hall then scoot closer to the desk, trying to see what Miss Hannah wrote about us.

Gershom flips the pages. They are attached at the top. I notice last year's report cards. He flips past doctors' visit forms and potential foster parent forms. Finally, on the last page, scribbled in red ink at the bottom, is our mother's name and address: *Stephanie Yanez, Auburn University, Auburn, Alabama. See Jontray Greene*.

Gershom and I look at each other. Auburn, *Alabama*?

Before either of us can form a more coherent thought, we hear steps in the hallway. It sounds like someone is banging their bag into the wall with every step.

"Quick—put it back!" I whisper. I dash to the door to see who's coming. "It's Miss Hannah!"

I hear Gershom's chair squeak just as Miss Hannah's bag smashes into the doorway.

I back up from the door trying not to look guilty, and Gershom gives Miss Hannah an innocent smile. "How ya doin',

Miss Hannah? Fancy meeting you here." He stands up and inches toward the door.

Miss Hannah drops her bag on her desk and wiggles her finger at us. "Hold on right there, young'un. I'm driving you to school. You can tell me what you were doing in here on the way." And with that, she leads the way out the door.

I look at Gershom and hiss, "Foolproof? You forgot about the exit plan!"

He shrugs his shoulders and whispers back, "Don't worry. Meet me at the library at lunch time. I have another plan."

I groan. *Another* plan? Because obviously the first one worked out so well! Crazy ideas aside, though, I want to know if we're still planning to find our mother, now that we know she lives in Alabama.

3 – Gershom's Pink Bicycle

I followed Miss Hannah and Jasmine out to the parking lot and into Miss Hannah's car. Jasmine was right—I hadn't thought through the exit strategy well enough. But no matter. I didn't have time to beat myself up over it. Another plan was coming together in my head and going to school fit in. Since our mother lived in Alabama, fifty dollars and some odd change wasn't going to be enough for bus fare, and we couldn't walk. We didn't have bicycles, but maybe some kids at school would sell us theirs.

I was so obsessed thinking about our transportation that I hadn't even noticed when we arrived at school. Miss Hannah had lectured, well, sermonized really, the entire way to school. I hadn't heard one word. However, before we hopped out, Miss Hannah turned to look me straight in the eye, even though she knew I had trouble maintaining eye contact.

"I don't know what you were doing in my office this morning, since you refused to say, but you two better behave yourselves in school today. I'll see you this afternoon. Gershom? Understand?"

We both nodded our heads, but I couldn't meet Miss Hannah's gaze. "Yes, ma'am." I pushed Jasmine out. No time to delay.

Jasmine waved at Miss Hannah. "Goodbye! And thank you for everything you've done!"

Miss Hannah looked confused but waved back and drove away. I turned to Jasmine.

"You can't tell people we're leaving! Tell your friends goodbye, but don't make it sound like it's a forever goodbye."

"So, we are going to Alabama?" Jasmine hitched her backpack higher on her shoulder. I draped my arm across her back and nodded. She thought for a minute and asked the hundred-dollar question, "How are we going to get there?"

"Ask around and see if anyone has a bike for sale. If they ask, say you have twenty bucks to pay. And don't forget—meet at the library at lunch time," I reminded her. "It's gonna be okay. You'll see. Now go to class and act normal."

The next three hours crawled by. Our middle school wasn't the biggest school in the state, but we had our fair share of students. Between every class, I spread the word that I was looking for two bikes. By the time the first lunch bell rang, I still had no leads on transportation. Maybe Jasmine had had better luck.

I made my way to the library and saw Jasmine standing there with two older boys, one on each side of her. My fists clenched tight, but I couldn't afford a meltdown right now. Remembering my therapy session from last week, I took a deep breath and closed my eyes, letting my emotions wash over me. I opened my eyes and glared at the boys.

"Jaz? You okay?"

Jasmine smiled at me. "These guys have some bikes they want to show you. You remember Matt? He's my friend Mary's brother."

"Oh. Well, okay." I realized I did know Matt; he was in my pre-algebra class. He had gone to eighth grade at the beginning of the year, but after two weeks, the teachers sent him back to seventh grade. He wasn't too much of a bully, just bigger than the rest of us. The other boy was probably his friend.

I tipped my head at Matt. "You have bikes?"

Matt shuffled his feet. "Yeah, Mary said Jasmine could have her old bike. This here's Jones. He's my neighbor. Mary said you needed two bikes, and Jones has an old one of his cousin's from last summer."

"Sounds good. Where are they?"

Jones pointed to the subdivision across from the school. "At home in our garages. You wanna see them now or after school?"

"We can't miss our bus after school," Jasmine said.

I opened my mouth to contradict her and Matt quirked an eyebrow at her, but I shut my mouth, shrugged, and headed through the library toward the back exit. Only the janitor and the detention kids used the exit behind the library, so there were no guards to stop us from leaving school property. A couple minutes later we stood facing two white houses, separated by the iconic picket fence. Jasmine and I stayed on the sidewalk while Matt and Jones went around back and brought out their bikes.

"Here you go!" proclaimed Matt. They wheeled the bikes up to the fence and parked them for us to look at. Two pink bicycles. Pink, both of them! One was light pink with flower stickers plastered all over it and pink streamers dangling from the handlebars. The other one was slightly smaller with a basket attached to the front handlebars. And it was neon pink. You could see it coming a mile away. I looked up at Matt.

"Seriously? They're both pink!" I looked at Jones sideways. "I guess that cousin of yours is a girl?"

He chuckled. "My cousin Sophia would go riding with Mary almost every day last summer. But she's going to her other cousins' house this summer, so they'll get her a new bike."

"So?" Matt prompted. "Beggars can't be choosers. You want 'em or what?" He looked at Jones, and they slapped their knees, laughing hard.

"Very funny," I huffed. No matter how much I didn't like it, Matt was right. I didn't have a choice if I wanted a bike today. "How much?"

Jones asked, "How much you got?"

I glanced at the pink bikes and looked at Jasmine. She shrugged. Good, she hadn't told them how much I had yet. I reached my hand into my pocket, trying to separate the ten-dollar bills in my envelope.

"Ten bucks."

Matt laughed a short "HA!" and I quickly added to my statement:

"Each. Ten bucks each." I pulled out my envelope of money and removed two tens. No way was I chancing pulling out my twenty.

"Here." I waved one bill at Jones and one at Matt. "Thanks, man."

"All right then." Matt slapped Jones on the back. "Let's go, Jones. See you around, Gershom!"

The two boys headed back to school, and I turned my focus to Jasmine and our new pink bikes. I grabbed the streamers, intent on pulling them off—I may not have a choice in riding a pink bike, but I sure wasn't going to parade myself down the East Coast with streamers flying behind me.

"Can I have the streamers?" Jasmine jumped over to me and put her hands on mine to stop me from ripping them.

Poor kid. She finally had a placement that wasn't terrible and here I was pulling her away. I sighed, knowing her placement would eventually turn out the same as all the others, and wishing I had more to offer her than year-old streamers.

"Of course, Jaz. The streamers are all yours."

"Oh, yay!" Jasmine bent over and gently pulled the streamers off. She turned, tied them onto the neon bike, and grinned at me. "You thought you were going to have to ride the neon pink bike, didn't you?"

I laughed. For the first time today, I didn't feel like the weight of the world sat on my shoulders. "Come on, cheeky little sister. Let's eat, then split. In Binghamton I'll find an atlas so we can figure out how to get to Alabama."

We hopped on our new bikes and passed Matt and Jones on our way back to school. After stashing the bikes behind the library, we walked in, arm in arm, ready to load our pockets with as much food as we could pilfer and begin our greatest adventure. I had already decided—getting to see our mother at the end of this was worth riding a pink bicycle, but I sure was glad I didn't have to ride the neon one. I just hoped we really would see our mother at the end of this—and that she wanted us.

4 — Jasmine's New Dog

My feet hurt. We haven't even been pedaling for five miles—at least, I don't think we've gone five miles yet. How can I be this tired already? I'm never going to make it to Alabama!

"Jasmine!" Gershom calls to me over his shoulder. "Keep up."

I nod. He can't see me from up there, but I'm trying to conserve my strength. Left foot, right foot. Left foot, right foot. This is ridiculous.

"Gershom, wait!" I pant. I pull off the shoulder and tumble onto the grass.

Gershom stops, turns around, and walks his bike back to where I am. "Jaz, there's a gas station just up ahead. Do you see it?"

"We don't need gas; we're riding bikes," I say between huffs.

Gershom laughs. "Not for gas. I'm gonna buy a map. I'm hoping it won't be too expensive. We don't need a fancy one; if it's got the highways on it, we'll be fine. Do you want to wait here?"

I nod and hold out my water bottle I got at lunch. "Can you fill this up for me at the water fountain?"

Gershom grabs it and with a warning to stay right here, he pedals off. Like I want to go anywhere! I lay back and stare at the trees. The leaves are a vibrant green, and the wind is rustling through them. The next thing I know, Gershom is kicking my foot.

"Get up, Sleepyhead. I got the map and your water. I want to get a good ways into Pennsylvania before we stop for the night."

Gershom helps me up, and we hop back on our bikes.

My power nap—that is what Mrs. Whitman always calls a super short nap—woke me up, so now I'm keeping up with Gershom without any trouble. It feels nice to know that every pedal, every bicycle step, gets me that much closer to my mother. I wonder what she looks like. I wonder if I will like her.

"Look out!" Gershom yells.

I screech my brakes and barely avoid slamming into him. His bike is stopped at an angle to the road, and I look up just in time to see a blue car sail right through a red light and crash into a black van in the intersection.

"Oh, Gershom! Do you think they're okay?" I want to run out there to make sure no one got hurt. Several cars have already stopped, and a small crowd gathers around the mangled vehicles.

Gershom grabs my arm. "Just wait a minute. See what happens." He darts behind a car on this side of the street, and I slide in beside him. A teenage girl spills out of the van, babbling something about it not being her fault.

The driver of the little blue car swings open his door, and a puppy skitters away from him. I kneel down and softly call to the puppy, and he wiggles his way through the mess of cars to me. As I cradle him in my arms, I hear the man complaining about the dog.

"Where'd that scamp get off to now? I can't just leave it on the side of the road!"

I peek around the car we're hiding behind. The teenager asks which direction it went, and I tighten my arms around my dog.

"Ach, I don't know. It was the last one I was trying to get rid of, but I hate just abandoning it."

Gershom eyes me, and I give him a look that says it's too late. This dog is mine now. He sighs. "Well, let's go then."

My big gray-blue eyes shine bright against my dark skin. They get him every time. He thinks he's a tough guy, but underneath I know he's a big softie.

"Should I let him know I'll take good care of this puppy?"

Gershom considers the scene in front of us. "No, better not get involved. As soon as the police get here, that man will forget all about the dog. And I don't want to be here when they arrive!"

"Okay," I say, hugging the puppy closer. He has floppy little ears, and his strong little tail is so cute. I brush my fingers down his short, cropped fur.

In response, he licks my nose. His tongue feels like sandpaper. That's what I'll call him! "Isn't Sandy just so cute?"

Gershom rolls his eyes. "It's a good thing your bike has the basket. I'm not carrying around no dog!"

I smile as I take my jacket out of my backpack and put it in my basket.

"You know, by the time we get to the Pennsylvania border, your jacket will be messed up. That dog's gonna do his business right there." Gershom shakes his head and starts pedaling back to the sidewalk.

I stoop down and pull up a couple handfuls of grass to replace my jacket under the dog. I hadn't thought of what Sandy might do in a few minutes. I get him situated and notice the trip suddenly feels shorter. I glimpse at Sandy every now and then as I pedal. Is Someone looking out for me? I shrug and just enjoy Sandy's company for now.

5 — Newman's Corner, NY

Hannah Summers sighed as she walked down the hallway at OCFS. She had so many kids to worry about, and today she had to find new homes for two of her boys, Gershom and Justin. They weren't bad kids; the latest placement hadn't been vetted like it should have, so it really was no wonder it had ended badly.

Hannah closed her office door and sat at her desk. Her laptop buzzed to life, and she looked around the room trying to figure out why Gershom and Jasmine would have been in here this morning. Her eyes fell to the filing cabinet, and the bottom drawer was ajar just a bit. Could they have been snooping in their file for something?

Patricia knocked on Hannah's door, and Hannah waved her in.

"Hey, Pat, thanks for the call this morning. Do you know what those kids were after?"

Patricia shook her head. "Sorry. I just thought it was strange. Here are the forms you printed off earlier. I found them in the copy room and thought I'd bring them down to you."

Hannah reached over for the stack of papers. "Thanks so much. I gotta find a new home for the boy that was here this morning. Such a shame. Good kids, but they're going to spend their whole life in foster care and won't have any family when they're up and grown."

Patricia shook her head. "Sounds like most of the teenagers we have, though. Oh, that's my phone! Better scoot!"

Hannah's door had barely closed again when her phone rang, too. "Hello?"

"Hannah Summers? You're still Jasmine's social worker, right?"

"Yes." Hannah sat up straight. She recognized Stacy Whitman's voice right away. Maybe Stacy knew what Jasmine and her brother were up to this morning. "What seems to be the matter?"

Stacy's voice came across the line thin and wobbly. "Jasmine didn't come home after school. When I phoned the office, they said she skipped all her classes after lunch. I'm worried something's happened to her!"

Hannah's eyes darted to her filing cabinet again. "Mrs. Whitman, stay by the phone. I need to check out a couple things, and I'll call you right back. Don't worry, okay? I'm sure she's fine. She's probably out with her brother, exploring the town or something." As Hannah said it, she knew it sounded preposterous, but it was a better thought than the alternative.

Hannah hung up and opened the bottom drawer of the cabinet. Sure enough, the Yanez kids' file looked haphazardly stuffed in. Most of the paperwork in here would be boring to kids, but if Gershom knew he was getting a new home today, maybe he came looking for something specific. Hannah flipped the pages all the way to the end, and then sat there staring with her jaw open.

Stephanie Yanez, Auburn University, Auburn, Alabama. Of course! Just the other day, Hannah had informed Ms. Gail that Gershom's mother still lived in Auburn. Auburn, New York, was about fifteen minutes north, but when Gershom found out his mother lived in Auburn, Alabama, would he still think it was a good idea to take off after her? Knowing the way Gershom reasoned, Hannah thought he probably would.

Hannah pulled up her internet and did a quick search for a route from Newman's Corner to Auburn, Alabama. She made the route go on secondary roads only, but either way she saw that the kids would have to go through Binghamton. She zoomed in on the highway and noted the various gas stations along the way.

She snatched up her desk phone and dialed the police station. She tapped her pen nervously as it rang.

"Newman's Corner Police Station, please hold!"

"No, wait—!" Hannah started, then let out her breath as symphony music filled her ear. With each passing minute, those kids were getting further away. She didn't have time to hold!

"I'm sorry for the wait. How may I direct your call?" The receptionist's voice came through again.

"I need to speak with Officer Baxter please. It's an emergency!" Hannah gripped the phone with both hands.

"I'm sorry, Office Baxter took early retirement last week. Can I connect you to his replacement, Officer Beech?"

Hannah blinked. "Uh, yes, please."

"Okay, one moment."

A few seconds of hold music, then Officer Beech's voicemail clicked on. Hannah sighed but left a message, urging him to call her back immediately on her cell.

She grabbed her cell phone and keys out of her purse, and clutching her notebook and the kids' file, she rushed out of her office.

"I'll be back on Monday, Pat! I have some errands to run." Hannah waved at Pat as the front office door banged shut. Hannah was on a mission. As much as she hoped she was wrong, she had a feeling she knew exactly where Gershom and Jasmine were headed.

6 — Gershom's Fears

"Woo-hoo!" I heard Jasmine behind me celebrating, but we had just started out, so I thought it might be premature to be super happy about anything. A minute later, she pedaled fast to catch up to me.

"What was that all about?" I asked.

"Didn't you see the sign? We're in Pennsylvania! That was so fast! Are we gonna be in Alabama by tomorrow? Do you think we could stop soon? I have to go to the bathroom." Jasmine's new dog was sleeping in her basket, but that didn't stop Jasmine from being excitably loud.

I nodded. “Yes, I saw the sign, and I’m happy we’re in Pennsylvania, too. But we lived close to the border. It will be a while before we cross another state border. I’m guessing maybe two weeks until we get to Alabama. And if you can wait a little bit, there’s a gas station about a mile up ahead.”

Even as I said it, I wondered about how smart it was to show our faces at every gas station from Newman’s Corner to Auburn. Surely someone would look for us. I didn’t want to get caught one day into our journey.

Jasmine agreed then slowed her pedaling so we were in single file again. Now that we were on the road and in another state already, I knew I had to figure out what we should do for sleeping. I had read that most people on the run with no money slept in their cars, but that obviously wouldn’t work for us. Maybe we could find a bridge. Another yell from Jasmine derailed my thoughts.

“What now, Jaz?” I turned around to see her pointing at the gas station we had just passed. “Oops!” We both turned our bikes around and headed back. “Run in quick. I’ll stay out here with our bikes and your dog.”

I picked Sandy up and let him explore the strip of grass between the gas station parking lot and the highway. While I waited for Jasmine and Sandy, I pulled out my money envelope to do a little figuring. The bikes had cost twenty dollars, and the map took another seven, so that left me with just over twenty-three dollars. To make that last two weeks, we could only spend, well, less than a dollar per day, for each of us. How would we live on half a hamburger for an entire day?

Jasmine came out and asked me, “What time is it?”

I checked my watch, then looked west at the setting sun. It wouldn’t set for another two hours, probably, but stopping for the map plus that accident in Binghamton had slowed our progress.

“It’s 5:30.” My stomach gurgled, reminding me that right about now Justin and I would have been in our room with our TV dinners, wolfing down the food before Marcus returned from wherever he normally spent his days; except, I reminded myself, we were going back to Miss Hannah today after school to find another home, so who knows where I would be.

“Can I have a roll for supper? I managed to fit five rolls in my pockets; aren’t you proud of me?” Jasmine held up a roll with a sliver of ham. I had forgotten about the rolls!

“Good idea. Eat it slow, so you don’t get sick. Do you have enough water?” I picked out one of my rolls and took a bite.

“Yes, Mom. Seriously, I should call you Mrs. Whitman. It was nice coming from her, though. You’re just my brother.” Jasmine plopped onto the ground, seemingly annoyed by my concern.

“You know I’d do anything for you? More so than Mrs. Whitman, even.” I sat down next to her. “I’ve seen the way adults are, and getting a check from Social Services every month for us isn’t enough to make them love us. But I’ll always love you, Jaz.”

Jasmine shoved my shoulder. "I know, silly brother. I love you, too. But I was with the Whitmans for almost a year. I don't think it was about the money to them."

"Come on," I stood up and motioned for Jasmine to do the same. Enough of this talk about the Whitmans and how wonderful they were. "We can still get a little farther south before stopping for the night."

We hopped back on our bikes and rode in silence for a while. My thoughts were swirling in my head so much that I didn't notice it getting dark.

"Gershom! Stop!" For the third time that day, Jasmine's yell interrupted me. When I stopped my bike, I realized the sun was almost over the horizon.

"It's all right," I told Jasmine, pedaling again. "I'm planning to sleep under the next bridge we come to." As the words left my mouth, a bridge appeared around the corner. "See, here's one now. How about this one?" Bridges seemed pretty common around here, so I wasn't too surprised that another one popped up so quickly.

We pulled our bikes up under the bridge and as a truck rumbled overhead, I realized this one was an interstate overpass. The concrete was like a hill that met the underside of the bridge. We climbed up to the top corner and sat facing the highway we had just been on. I pulled out my jacket and laid it on the ground, and Jasmine copied me. Her dog ran around for a few minutes, playing in what little grass could grow under the bridge, before turning circles and promptly going to sleep.

I spread my map out, then realized the sun had gone down too much for me to read it now. In the morning I'd look for a creek or lake.

"How much should I eat?" Jasmine asked.

I looked at her food stash. "I don't know. How hungry are you?"

"Pretty hungry." Her stomach growled, and I laughed. My stomach answered, and Jasmine laughed.

"Well, if it takes us two weeks to get there, and we each buy a hamburger every day, that means fourteen days times two people equals twenty-eight, but today is almost gone and factor in some luck in there somewhere, minus the twenty-three dollars I have—we'll need our rolls to last three days. Or something like that."

A tear escaped Jasmine's eye and made a dirty track down her cheek. "But I'm more hungry than that."

I patted Jasmine's back. She only used bad grammar when she was upset. "It's okay, Jaz, you can eat two rolls. Maybe tomorrow we can find a library and look up soup kitchens on our route or something. Then we wouldn't have to worry about food. We'll fill up our bottles at the water fountain in the library. Just leave the worrying to me, okay?"

Jasmine hiccupped and nodded and drank most of the rest of her water. "I guess I'd better leave some for Sandy tomorrow." She hiccupped again and curled up next to her dog.

Tomorrow, I hoped, would be a better day—one filled with warm meals that ended without tears. I didn't actually think I could find a soup kitchen—or that they'd let us in without an adult—but I was too tired to keep thinking about it now. I looked up at the stars just coming out of hiding and wondered if life was supposed to be this difficult, or if the trouble I felt on my shoulders was all my own doing. I curled up next to Jasmine; my last thought before drifting off was about how nice it would be to finally have someone else worry about stuff for me, although I wasn't too sure a mom who abandoned toddlers to foster care would want to take on preteens.

7 — Binghamton, NY

Hannah pulled into the first gas station parking lot after passing the Binghamton city sign. She turned her engine off and sat for a moment, wondering what would possess two kids to attempt a trip down the entire East Coast. Hannah knew that, like many foster kids, Gershom and Jasmine had never been given their own bikes, so she was hoping they were on foot, meaning she could catch up to them fairly quickly. She pulled out their pictures from their file and headed inside.

The bell above the door clanged as Hannah made her way to the counter. She nodded to the man at the register and slid her pictures over to him.

"Have you seen these kids?" she asked.

The man squinted toward the pictures and shook his head. "Sorry," he rasped. He hacked a cough and shrugged, then went back to organizing the rows of gum on the counter.

Hannah sighed and realized this might be a little more difficult than she had originally anticipated. "Thanks," she threw back as the bell clanged again. She got in her car and marked one stop off her list.

"One down and only seventeen more to go," she muttered to herself.

At the next stop, she replayed her actions from before, but this time the man had a different answer.

"Oh yeah, I saw the boy. He came in here a couple a hours ago. Filled up some water bottles and bought a map. Ripped it in half and threw away most of the United States. I thought that was peculiar. But it was a big map to start with. If I was gonna carry it a ways and only needed a section, I'd have ripped it up, too."

Hannah's initial excitement grew with every word the man spoke. Then her heart plunged to her feet.

"Saw him go out and get on his bike. Another peculiar thing—it was pink! But hey, I don't judge." The man held up his hands like someone might shoot him for thinking pink was peculiar.

"Wait—his bike?" Hannah interrupted. "Did you see this girl out there too? Did she have a bike?" Hannah held her breath, hoping the man had been mistaken.

"Uh, yep. She was there and had a bike too. Hers was bright pink." The man nodded his head vigorously.

Hannah's shoulders slumped. If the kids had bikes, they would've gotten a lot farther south by now. She didn't have the time or resources to jet off on a cross-country trip after them. She thought of her options on her way home. It was too late now to go back to the office, but she decided that first thing Monday morning—after calling the police station again if Officer Beech hadn't called her back over the weekend—she would look up Jontray Greene's number at Auburn University and call him, warning him that two children were on their way and to keep an eye out for them.

Of course, as busy as she was, when Monday rolled around, other issues demanded her attention and Gershom and Jasmine inadvertently slipped from her "urgent" list onto her "when I have spare time" list.

8 — Jasmine and Sandy

A loud rumble over my head wakes me up. For a minute, my brain is confused, but then the memories of yesterday flood my mind. Gershom said today we would find a soup kitchen and eat to our hearts' content. I'm not worried about needing a rest from the bikes; I rode all the time when I lived with the Whitmans. They let me use their daughter's bike—she left it at their house when she moved away to college.

"Jasmine, your dog."

I sit up and look around. Gershom is lying on his jacket, and sometime in the night Sandy crawled to lie on top of him. I laugh and pick Sandy up, waking him. He wiggles, and I put him down to explore.

"Time to get up anyway, Gersh. It's breakfast time."

We both stand up and start collecting our things. I'm so hungry I don't bother asking—I just shove half a roll in my mouth and start chomping. A loud blaring HONK! startles me and I drop the rest of my roll.

Gershom picks up my roll and brushes it off. "Don't be scared. It's just traffic on the interstate. Are you ready?" He twists his map around, checking it with a frown. "It looks like there's a town about fifteen minutes up the road. We should be able to find a library there."

I call to Sandy and put him in my bike basket. He whines so I give him the rest of my roll. My stomach felt a little queasy at the thought of finishing it after it fell on the ground anyway.

I'm just starting to get hungry again—hungry for an actual breakfast—when we pass a sign welcoming us to a town with a population of 256 ½ people. That is very strange.

"Hey Gersh, how do they figure half a person on their population sign?" I ask. Maybe someone is on their deathbed. Maybe someone's not born yet. Maybe someone doesn't have any legs, so they are considered half a person.

Gershom shrugs. "It's a mystery," he calls back to me. "Look! There's a cookout!"

We ride up to an oil change place and consider the sign out front. "Free hot dogs for lunch every Saturday until September." Lunch is still a long way off, but we pull up to the front door intent on asking for food now. Gershom gets off his bike and motions that he'll be right back.

"Why do I always have to be the one to wait outside?" I ask Sandy. He just looks up at me, his tongue hanging out of his mouth.

A couple minutes later, he comes back out, a huge grin on his face. "The guy in there said we could have a hot dog now if we wanted. I don't know how long they'll keep in our backpacks, but I figure we can take some to last us all day today, at least." We wheel our bikes over to the barbeque pit. "I'll get some hot dogs for you if you want to run in to the bathroom."

"Okay. Don't forget to get a couple for Sandy," I tell him as I walk back to the building. I giggle, thinking of my dog eating hot dogs. On my way back outside, I wave at the owner and thank him for breakfast. I whisper, "And lunch and supper."

As soon as I get to my bike, a man in a uniform covered in grease charges out the door, waving his arms and flapping a rag at us. Gershom and I look at each other in fear. I grab two water bottles from the cooler next to the grill, throw them in my basket with Sandy, and we jump on our bikes and peel out of there.

After ten minutes of riding, we finally slow down. I tell Gershom, "One stop sign. That was a small town! You don't think anyone's coming after us for taking all the hot dogs, do you?"

Gershom laughs. "Nah. I don't know what that guy was coming out to say, but did you see the look on his face? Like he had just eaten a lemon. I didn't want to stick around to find out what was on his mind."

We pedal at a nice pace for a couple hours. When we stop for lunch, Gershom spreads out his map. "It looks like there's a creek that will cross our path just up ahead, maybe in an hour. We could stop and wash off a little and fill our bottles up again."

"Sounds like a plan," I agree. "Let's hurry and eat. I can't wait to wash my face and arms. And brush my teeth! Do you think we'll have time to go wading, too?"

Gershom shrugs. "We can probably take half an hour or so. I don't want to spend the rest of the day there. Just don't get your hopes up too much. It looks like a minuscule creek on this map."

"Minuscule? What is that, full of muscles?"

Gershom snorts at me and waves the map around. "Little, tiny, small, mini—get it? Mini-scule?"

"Mm," I grunt. "But a creek, no matter what size on the map, is bound to have enough water to wade, right? I mean, it's not like I want an Olympic-sized swimming pool." I figure Gershom's just being negative because he doesn't want to stop at all.

Gershom shrugs at me, and we continue on our bikes. After an hour of riding, I hear a trickling sound.

"Hey, it's the creek!" I yell to Gershom. We pull off the highway and walk our bikes down to the bank. My shoulders sag as I look at the tiny stream. "Where's the rest of the water?"

Gershom shakes his head. "I had a feeling it would be like this. They probably haven't had rain in a while. Smaller creeks like this tend to dry out quickly with no rain. At least we can wash our hands and Sandy can play in the water for a few minutes."

I lift Sandy out of my basket, and he has a blast, yapping and bouncing back and forth in the creek. Gershom and I wash our hands and splash a tiny bit of water on our faces. I rinse my toothbrush out in a mostly clean, swirling puddle formed by two rocks and a stick. The birds chirp all around us, and the breeze blows softly through the branches overhead.

"This is nice," I say, sitting in the grass and leaning back to look at the sky. "Can we just live here instead?"

Gershom grunts. "What did that paper say at Miss Hannah's office again? I've been thinking about the names that were listed."

"Stephanie Yanez—that would be our mother, right? Same last name as ours."

"Right, but there was another name, a man's name. It was after Auburn, Alabama. Jamarcus Greene?" Gershom walks over to the creek with his bottle. I fish mine out of my backpack.

"Hm," I think. I do remember another name, but Jamarcus doesn't sound right. "Was it Johntey Greene?" Gershom walks back over to me, and I hand him my bottle with a grin. He grins back and takes my bottle.

"Yeah, I think you're right. Johntey sounds more like it. Oh! Jontray Greene." Gershom wheels to facc me and pumps his fist in the air. "I remembered!"

I laugh. "I guess when something is important, it's easier to remember. I wonder who Jontray Greene is."

"Yeah, me too. I wonder why he was written in our file. I've never heard his name before." Gershom hands me my filled bottle and continues, "We'd better get going. We'll never find out who he is if we stay here all day."

I agree and catch Sandy. "Too bad I don't have a leash. Sandy's all wet!"

"He'll dry off once we start pedaling down the road."

We make our way back to the road and head out again. This adventure is turning out to be fun. I get to spend all this time with my brother that ordinarily I wouldn't. I'm getting lots of exercise. And the best part is yet to come: seeing my mother at the end and figuring out who Jontray Greene is.

9 — Gershom's Name

Today marked our third day on this crazy journey. It didn't start out as a good day. When we woke up, we were soaking wet from a light rain that had begun during the night. We ate the last of our rolls from the cafeteria for breakfast before heading out. Three hours later we hadn't come across any towns, and the rain hadn't let up either. I was trying to stay positive, but I could tell Jasmine was having none of it.

"Gershom, why did we come out here? It's raining, we have no food, and I'm so cold being this wet. Even Sandy is miserable and hungry. What are we going to do?" She stopped her bike, gingerly took Sandy out of her basket, then knocked over her bike and huddled in a squat on the ground.

"Well, first get out of the road! What if someone comes and they're not paying attention?" I helped Jasmine onto the shoulder and checked my watch. It was already one-thirty, although it could have been five in the afternoon, what with all the clouds.

Jasmine grumbled, "There are no cars on the road. Isn't it Sunday? No one goes anywhere on Sunday."

At that moment, a semi-truck rumbled over the hill and passed us, driving straight through all the puddles and making us even wetter, if that was possible. As soon as it passed, I turned to Jasmine and gave her my look. She rolled her eyes at me.

"Yeah, yeah. So, a truck came, and it would have flattened me. At this rate—" Jasmine cut off her sentence to point at the truck. It had screeched to a halt several hundred yards ahead of us.

"It's okay, Jaz. I'll see what the problem is." I made sure she was safe, then I jogged up to where the trucker was getting out of his cab. His jeans looked new and his cowboy boots made sharp clicks when he walked. His shirt looked crisp and clean—not at all like what I imagined truckers would look like. Before I could ask him what the trouble was, he spoke.

"Everything all right with you kids? Is that your sister on the ground? Is she okay?" The man took off his big hat to run his hand through his hair. "It's pretty wet out here—what are you kids doing on the main road?"

I looked back at Jasmine. She was rubbing Sandy's fur scrunched up at his neck. I cleared my throat and spoke in as professional a voice as I could muster.

"Our mom accidentally left without us. We are just catching up to her."

I thought keeping it simple was the best option, but this man wanted details. Lots of details.

"How does a mom leave somewhere without her kids? And how far are you traveling? And why, for all that's good in the world, didn't you just call her to let her know?"

Jasmine piped up, "Oh, you'd be surprised at how often parents leave without their kids. It's a crime, really." She shook her head in disapproval.

"And my mom doesn't believe in phones," I added quickly, then I cringed at how that sounded. Who doesn't believe in phones?

The man settled his hat back on his head as he assessed us, and I could tell he knew we were keeping back major parts of our story.

"Hm, well, can I give you guys a ride somewhere? The police station, maybe?"

"No! I mean, not the police station. I know where we're going," I tried to assure him.

I also knew kids weren't supposed to take rides from strangers, but he seemed like a decent person, and we were already soaked. How could I know I could trust this guy? I decided to ask straight out, and based on his facial expression, I would know.

"How do I know you're not a serial kidnapper who sells kids on the black market?" I challenged him.

His face immediately broke into a grin. He slapped his knee and said, "Well, if I ever kidnapped a kid and sold him, I don't think Someone would be very happy with me," and he pointed up to the sky. "My name's Paul. I'm headed to Virginia Beach, and I'll take you as far as you want to go."

I rolled my eyes. I wasn't sure Paul's "Someone" really cared about what happened with us, but a ride was a ride, just the same. "Hang on a minute," I told him, and I jogged back to tell Jasmine everything Paul had just said.

"Yes! Tell him yes, we'll take a ride." Jasmine's eyes begged me to save her from the rain. Sandy pawed at my leg and whined.

"Okay, get your bike up and let's go." I still wasn't one hundred percent sure this was a good idea, but I thought maybe if Paul believed in a higher power in Heaven, maybe He could protect us. If I knew from whom specifically to ask for protection, I would be on my knees right now. As it was, I directed "please help us" thoughts toward the clouds as we wheeled our bikes up to Paul, hoping God hadn't heard my earlier dismissal of Him.

While I talked to Jasmine, Paul had gotten an umbrella and a towel out from his cab. He handed me the open umbrella and said, “Hold this over your bike while I wipe it off. No sense in getting the inside wetter than it needs to be.” To Jasmine he said, “Take your jacket off and hop up in there. There’s a newspaper on the floor where you can put your dog. Reach on in the back and grab yourself another towel if you want.”

We made quick work of drying off the bikes and getting them inside. I climbed in next to Jasmine, and Paul jumped in next to me, shaking the umbrella and stowing it in the back.

Jasmine jabbed me in the side and motioned with her eyes at the cross dangling from the mirror. I nodded. Then she grabbed my head and pulled it close to her face.

“Ask him if he has anything to eat,” she whispered.

I nodded again, and my stomach growled. Paul laughed.

“I guess you kids are hungry, huh? There’s leftover pizza in the back.” He jabbed back with his thumb, and I twisted around to look. A fast-food pizza box lay on the floor, a stack of napkins peeking out from underneath. My mouth watered just looking at that box.

“What are you waiting for?” Jasmine screeched. “Get the pizza! I’m starving.”

Before I could unbuckle, Jasmine scrambled over the back of the seat and plopped herself down next to the pizza. “It’s still warm, Gersh.” She lifted the lid and closed her eyes. “Oh, it smells heavenly.”

"Hey, pass me a piece already." My stomach growled again. Rain always made me hungrier than normal; even Abigale had noticed it. Every day that it rained when I was with them, Abigale made Marcus buy me an entire pizza. She always made sure I knew it was "coming out of my allowance," which I basically ignored because they never gave me any allowance to begin with.

Jasmine handed me a slice, and I took a bite. It *was* heavenly. It hadn't rained for a couple weeks in Newman's Corner, meaning it had been a while since I'd had pizza. It tasted better than I remembered.

Paul broke into my bliss. "Hey, I'm gonna say a quick prayer of thanks, all right?" He winked at me and touched the small gold cross hanging from his rearview mirror.

I snorted and swallowed. "Thanks? Thanks for what? Our mother abandoned us and left us to rot in foster care, it's pouring rain, and we have no food. What in there, exactly, are we supposed to give thanks for?"

"Gershom!" Jasmine's quiet rebuke jolted me out of my anger. In my outburst I'd completely forgotten that Paul didn't know the whole story behind where we were going.

Paul shook his head. "I figured there was more to the story." He rubbed his chin with one hand. "Are you sure you know what you're doing?"

"Yeah," I answered hesitantly.

Paul checked in his side mirror and changed lanes. "Why don't you tell me everything? Start at the beginning."

His tone of voice was unlike any adult's I had heard before, like he was genuinely interested and wanted to help.

After Jasmine and I told him our story, he chuckled. "Providence really has been watching over you two. You and your sister are healthy enough to ride bicycles quite a long distance, and you're smart enough to figure out your own way. Right now, you're riding in a dry cab eating hot pizza. I'd say those are definitely things to be thankful for."

Jasmine piped up from the back, "You know, Gershom, when I found Sandy, I wondered if maybe Someone hadn't put him there just for me to find. I've loved having Sandy along for the ride."

I shook my head at them both. "I doubt it. Haven't you ever heard of a coincidence?"

Paul asked, "Your name is Gershom, right? You know where that came from?"

I shrugged my shoulders and took another bite. I had honestly never given my name much thought past, "Who names their kid *Gershom*?"

Paul elaborated. "Gershom was the name of Moses' son, you know, in the Bible. God told Moses to go to a specific country, and on the way there, he kinda got sidetracked. His son was born in that strange country, so he named him 'Gershom,' which means 'stranger.' Moses wanted to remember, every time he looked at his son, that he was bound for a different land, and that where they were now wasn't their home. Maybe you were born somewhere that wasn't your mom's home."

I'd never heard that story before. "Did they get to that different land, the one that was supposed to be their home?"

"Nope. Well, Moses didn't. He disobeyed God, so God told him he couldn't go into the land. But other people got to go."

I frowned. That didn't sound like a story with a happy ending. "I'm sure my mom didn't name me after some random dude in the Bible, 'cause—no offense—but that sounds stupid. My story will have a much happier ending than that."

Paul pointed at a sign we were passing. "Maryland Welcomes You," it said.

"Hey, Jaz! We're in Maryland now. You missed the sign." I turned around to look at her. "Any more pizza left? I'm still hungry."

She opened the lid again. "One piece left. Here. So if we're in Maryland already, does that mean we will get to Alabama sooner?"

I nodded. "Yep, because we're in a truck now. I figure we're shaving off at least a day of our trip, maybe two. Let me check my map." I pulled my map out of my backpack and spread it out on my lap. Thankfully, the one thing I insisted on was a top-of-the-line backpack, and it had kept my map perfectly dry. I found where Pennsylvania and Maryland met and ran my finger down to Virginia.

"Where is it that you're going again?" I asked Paul.

"Virginia Beach. It's right next to the ocean."

I studied the map for a few minutes, trying to figure out where we needed to get off. "I think if you let us out at Richmond, that would be good. You'll go right toward the beach, and we'll go left toward Alabama."

Paul nodded. "Sounds good, kid. Now rest for a bit. We'll be in Richmond in a couple hours."

I checked on Jasmine—she was already sound asleep—and turned to gaze out the window. We'd gone from cold, hungry, wet, and alone to warm and dry, with full bellies and a stranger-turned-friend helping us out. Maybe I did have some things to be thankful for. Since Paul piqued my interest about my name, I was eager to meet my mother and ask why she had picked the name Gershom for me.

Paul turned on the radio, and I drifted off to sleep to the strains of someone singing about amazing grace.

10 — Jasmine's Reminder

A strange voice is talking. It's loud and deep, like a man's voice. Gershom doesn't sound like this. Who is this, and what's so important that he feels the need to wake me up?

"Jasmine, wake up." Gershom's voice joins the stranger's.

I open my eyes. "I'm awake already. What's the big emergency?" I sit up, and when I see where I am, I remember. The stranger's voice belongs to Paul, the man giving us a ride in his truck. "Are we there yet?" I ask, stretching the sleep from my body.

Paul snorts. "Ah, famous last words from a kid. My little sister always used to ask me that when I took her on trips with me. Richmond is coming up; you need to let me know where to drop you off. There's a McDonald's right off the interstate. How do burgers for supper sound?"

I start to squeal, but then I see Gershom's face. I remember that we must stretch our money. He's probably trying to figure out if we can afford hamburgers yet. I smile when his face relaxes, and he smiles back.

"Yippee! Hamburgers!" I bounce in my seat. The sun is just beginning to set, pouring in streaks of red and orange through my window. The colors remind me of ketchup and mustard, and my mouth waters in anticipation of those yummy condiments I'll put on my burger.

"Here we are kids," Paul announces as we pull in the parking lot. There is a big dome play area, and for a second, I contemplate asking if I can play after I eat. Gershom will probably want to get out of the city before stopping for the night, meaning we'll have to get moving soon.

Paul says, "We can leave your bikes in my cab until you're ready to leave. That way no one will steal them."

When we get inside, he tells us to freshen up in the bathroom while he orders for us. I skip down the hallway, more than ready to wash my hands, but dreading what my hair must look like. Thankfully, my curls aren't too flattened. They could use a comb for sure, and some oil for the ends, but I guess a comb and oil aren't as important as a toothbrush.

When we come out of the bathroom, Paul waves at us from a table. He holds out two empty cups and says, "I didn't know what you wanted to drink. You can choose whatever you want."

I grab my empty cup and push all the buttons on the soda dispenser. I taste my strange concoction and grimace. Gershom laughs at my face. He puts Sprite in his cup. I shudder. Sprite is just as bad as everything else mixed together.

We enjoy a hot supper, starting with a prayer from Paul. Gershom keeps his eyes open, but I think it's a nice prayer. During supper, I ask Paul about the necklace hanging from his rearview mirror.

"Oh that," Paul says. He gets a faraway look in his eye and smiles. "My grandma gave me that just before she died. She was always going on about Heaven and Jesus, but when I was a kid, I never listened. Then when I was a teenager, my dad died, and I started asking my grandma questions about God and Heaven."

Gershom pipes up, "The same God that didn't let Moses in his land?"

I glare at my brother, but Paul answers, "The one and the same. Turns out God has this thing about not letting sin into Heaven, and the deal with Moses is a good picture for us. He sinned and wasn't allowed in. You see, everyone is born a sinner, so in order to get to Heaven, we need our sin taken away. We can't do that ourselves, so God sent His Son Jesus to die on a cross and take the sin of the whole world onto Himself. Three days later he rose up from the dead! Now all we have to do is ask Him to forgive us and trust that He is enough and BAM! We'll end up in Heaven when we die."

Gershom looks like he wants to roll his eyes at the fantastical story—a dead man, coming to life again after three days! It does seem far-fetched, so I ask Paul for clarification. "Okay, you mean He was dead. And then He was alive again? How is that even possible?"

Paul chuckles. "It's hard for us to understand sometimes, but God is so powerful, and with Him, nothing is impossible."

I "hmm" at that and chew on my burger. We let the conversation drop, and soon we finish eating. When we get our bikes and backpacks, I give Sandy my last bite of hamburger.

"Thank you, Mr. Paul, for the ride and the pizza and the burgers and, I guess that's all." I wave at him, then focus on getting Sandy ready for more riding. I hear Gershom's goodbye to our stranger-friend.

"Well, Paul, that was an interesting story about that Gershom from the Bible. I'll honestly think about it, and what I have to be thankful for."

I notice he didn't say anything about the story of Jesus dying on the cross or coming back to life again. I peek at Paul to see him shaking his head. "There's so much more in the Bible than a boy with your name. That's just a small chapter in the story of God's love. When you get to Alabama, you should get yourself a Bible and read about it."

I think that's a good idea, although it's hard to imagine God so loving when my own mother and father abandoned me. But He did send His own Son to die for me, so that must mean that He *does* love me.

"Come on, Gersh, don't we need to go?" I need time alone to think about all this.

"Yeah, we need to go. Thanks again, Paul, for everything." Gershom gets on his bike and we start to pedal away when Paul yells at me.

"Jasmine! Wait!"

I turn around and pedal back to the truck. Paul is holding something. He opens his hand and the cross necklace dangles from his fingers. The light catches it and makes it shine. He grabs my hand and places it under the necklace.

"Here, I want you to take this. Every time you look at it, remember that God loves you and is looking out for you in ways you don't even realize."

I hold the necklace up to the evening sunshine streaming through the trees. As it spins, I notice one little diamond at the top of the cross, sparkling as it glistens in the light.

"It's beautiful. Thank you." I look at Paul with wonder. Why would anyone want to give away such a beautiful piece of jewelry? It reminds me of the part of Paul's story where God gave His Son to die for everyone in the world.

Paul tips his hat at me and hauls himself up into his cab. "Take care, now!" he yells just before slamming the door. The engine roars to life, scaring me. I slip the necklace into my jacket pocket and pedal fast to catch up to Gershom.

"Come on," I mutter to Gershom. He looks at me crooked, like he's itching to ask what Paul gave me. I need to think about everything a little more before I talk to anyone about it, though. How does God fit in with our "escape to Alabama" plan? How does He fit in with the "meeting our mother" plan? I watch as Gershom rides in front of me, and I wonder if he's thinking about where God fits into our plans, too

11 — Gershom's Test

The sun was setting. That meant that we needed to stop soon for the night, but I really wanted to get out of the city first. I weighed the pros and cons of it: stop now before it got too dark, but risk the dangers of the city, or press on through the night and its dangers to get to a safer stopping place. Either way didn't sound very smart. We stopped at a red light, and I turned to ask Jasmine her opinion.

WOOP! WOO-OOP! The flashing blue and white lights blinked at us and disappeared. A police car was first in line at the red light, and the passenger window whirred down.

"Hey kids, what are you up to? I saw you guys get your bikes out of that semi-truck. You look like you could use some help, maybe."

Jasmine grabbed my arm. I looked at her, and her eyes were wide and white. I cleared my throat and tried to make my voice sound strong. "Thanks, Officer, but that was our uncle. He was just passing through town, so we rode out to meet him for supper. Our bikes were in his truck because we didn't want anyone to steal them. We're headed home now."

Jasmine nodded her head furiously. I placed my hand on her shoulder to calm her down. "Yes, Officer. Uncle Paul. Supper of burgers. We're going home. This is my dog."

I squeezed her shoulder. She was out of control and rambling. If she didn't stop, she was going to get us in trouble. At the last minute, she tacked on the end of her speech,

"Thanks, Officer! Bye!"

The light turned green as she said that, and we both waved. The officer didn't look convinced, and his car barely moved an inch. His lights came on again, and the cars behind him started passing us. He called out to us,

"Why don't I give you a ride home? It's getting dark, you know."

I jumped to answer first. "Oh, that's okay. We just live around the corner. We'll be there in eight or nine minutes. Thanks, though!" And I pushed Jasmine out of the way and set off pedaling. *Eight or nine days*, I corrected in my head. It was true, we were heading home. Not the home we had grown up in, but the home where family was. And I figured if you went back enough generations, eventually Paul's family tree and our family tree crossed somewhere—where else would Jasmine have gotten her gray-blue eyes?—so while it was a stretch to call him our uncle, it also was not one hundred percent false. Maybe just ninety-nine percent false.

Just then, the policeman's radio squawked, and he turned from us to listen. After only two or three seconds, he flipped his siren on to match his lights and merged into traffic, finally allowing me to breathe.

"That was a close one!" Jasmine commented. "I thought for sure he was going to take Sandy away."

"Sandy? If he'd wanted to, he could have arrested us! We're just runaway kids, far from home." I shook my head. "Let's get out of here before he comes back."

In a few minutes, the bright lights of the city were behind us. The country sprang up almost right away once we got beyond the city limits, so we found a bridge with a nice field next to it and made camp for the night. Sandy and Jasmine found a semi-comfortable position and fell asleep almost right away. I had trouble finding sleep, though.

Out here, the stars were brighter. The rain had finally stopped and the clouds had cleared, leaving the air with a fresh summer feel to it. I thought back on the past couple of days. Finding our mother's address. Finding bicycles. Finding food and even a ride today.

I thought about Paul's cross and what he said about God looking out for us. Maybe he did have a point about that, but the anxiety and fear that had crept up my throat while talking to the police muddled my thoughts. As I got comfortable for the night, I tried to clear my head so I wouldn't be exhausted tomorrow.

The next morning, the sun shone bright and warm. I heard Jasmine's laughter before I even opened my eyes. I smiled, happy that she was happy. Today was a new day, full of promise and—

"AHHH!"

I bolted up at Jasmine's scream. The top of her head disappeared in the grass. I dashed over to where she was and skidded to a halt at the edge of a hole in the ground.

"Jasmine! Are you okay? What happened?" I called down. The hole had sharply slanted sides and was about ten feet deep and maybe five feet wide. Sandy trotted up to the edge of the hole across from me and whimpered.

Jasmine's voice came up clearly. "I'm fine. How's Sandy? Can you get me out of here?"

She was crazy to think of Sandy at a time like this, but then again, she thought of Sandy first in every situation we found ourselves in.

"Let me look around real quick. Are there branches sticking out of the sides of the hole you can climb on?" I was reluctant to leave Jasmine, but how could I get her out? I thought back to a movie I had watched once with Justin, just days after we arrived at Marcus and Abigale's. It was about three animals that travelled across the country in search of their human family. At the end of the movie, the animals fell in a hole and had to work together to get out.

Jasmine's voice drifted out of the ground, "No branches. It's too slick to climb up. I'm stuck!"

"Let me go check our stuff and I'll be right back!" I looked across at Sandy and said, "Stay here, boy."

I ran back to the bridge and frantically looked around. Jasmine wasn't hurt, so that was good. But she couldn't stay down there, and I couldn't exactly go find help. I dumped my backpack out, but I knew the map and extra cheeseburgers from last night would do us no good. I picked up my jacket and fingered the sleeve. An idea took root in my mind. I ran to Jasmine's backpack and pulled out her windbreaker. That leash Jasmine had wanted for Sandy would have come in handy now, but I thought maybe I could make do with our jackets.

I ran back to where Sandy was sitting. He was trying to howl, but his puppy voice just made him sound whiny. "It's okay, boy. We'll get her out. Everything will be all right."

I tied one of my sleeves to one of Jasmine's sleeves and called down to her, "I've got our jackets like a rope. I'll let down yours. Grab onto the sleeve, and I'll pull you up." I lay down so I would have less chance of being pulled into the hole and reached the jacket-rope down as far as I could.

"I can barely reach it, Gersh! Can you drop it a little further?"

I scooted closer to the opening and stretched down my arms as far as they would go. "Try now. It's as low as I can reach."

I felt a tug on the jacket, and then I slowly started to slide toward the opening.

"I got it!" Jasmine called.

"Yeah, hold on tight! I'll pull you up!" I braced my arms and slowly tried to stand, pulling the jackets with me.

"Oof!" I landed abruptly on my backside. I picked up the jacket-rope and noticed with dismay that Jasmine's jacket was missing. The sleeves must have come undone.

"Gershom!" Jasmine screamed.

I crawled to the opening. "I'm sorry, Jaz. I'll go look for something else I can use. Maybe there's an old rope or something by the bridge."

Jasmine's hope had turned to despair, and her sobs floated up to me. Determined to save my sister, I took off back toward the bridge. I hoped there was something I could use, because if not, I was all out of ideas. Paul's face flashed in my mind. Where was his God now, when we needed help the most? I looked up to the sky and shook my fist. I hated to admit it, but I was scared, and whenever I got scared, I got mad. I certainly didn't want to fight anyone, but a little consideration would be nice.

My hand dropped, and I fell to my knees, exhausted with trying to do it myself. "Please, it's my sister." The words barely escaped my lips when there was a canister fell out of the sky and landed at my feet. I jumped to my feet and looked up. Either life was very coincidental, or God answered prayers fast.

A second paint can was just tipping over the side of the bridge, and I hopped back so it didn't hit me. I watched as two more cans came rolling over the edge. I picked one up to find it half full. I grabbed another one. It was empty, and I tossed it aside. For Jasmine to keep her footing if she stood on several, I knew empty cans would be too flimsy. The other two were also empty, so I clambered up to the bridge, where the road was filled with paint cans, slowly rolling around. I looked up and down the road—no vehicle in sight. I found three more half full cans and half-carried, half-dragged all four back to the hole.

As tempting as it was to take credit for her rescue, I could not dispel the thought that God was taking care of us. I felt ashamed of my behavior earlier and whispered a quick "I'm sorry" toward Heaven. Then I got busy saving my sister.

12 — Jasmine's Double Rescue

Oh, what am I going to do? I look up and see Sandy's nose poking over the top.

"Sandy! Get back, puppy! I don't want you falling in here too."

The walls used to be dry dirt, but they and the floor are a bit muddy now, probably from yesterday's rain. The absence of the warm breeze from earlier this morning makes me feel cold now. I guess it's a good thing my jacket was the one that fell in here when the sleeves untied themselves. I slip my jacket around my shoulders and look at the sky again. Where is Gershom?

I put my hands in my pockets and feel something with my right hand. I wrap my fingers around something small and cold. The points press into my skin and I remember the necklace Paul gave me yesterday. I pull it out and dangle it in front of me. His words echo in my ears as I rub the diamond.

"Every time you look at it, remember that God loves you and is looking out for you in ways you don't even realize."

Just holding the cross in my hand gives me a small measure of comfort. I don't know much about God, but Paul seemed to think He's the answer to all my problems.

"God?" I whisper. I look around at my dirt prison, down at the muddy ground, and up to the bright blue sky. Nothing happens. I get a cold chill, and I clutch my necklace tighter. "God, are you there?" I ask louder. "It's me, Jasmine. I need help." Suddenly, I have a lump in my throat. I shake my head and try again.

"I know I can't expect You to help me out of this hole after I've ignored You my whole life. But I don't want to ignore You anymore. From my experiences of the past several days, I've realized that I can't do this without help. I know what I'm about to ask is a lot, but Paul says You love me. So—"

My hands are wet, and I look up again. No rain. Then I realize I'm crying. I wipe my tears away and raise my fist clutching the necklace. "Please, God! I'm sorry for my sin. I can't do this alone. Please forgive me! Please help me!"

The next instant, my heart feels so light I think I could almost float out of the hole. I laugh and caress the cross in my fingers. I look up once more and whisper, "Thank you!"

Gershom's head comes into view and he says, "Why are you saying thank you? I haven't rescued you yet! But I'm about to."

"Oh Gersh!" I call up. "God just rescued me! I'm so happy. You need to let him rescue you too!"

Gershom scrunches up his face. "Uh, okay. For now, though, let's get you out of this hole, shall we? Scoot over and flatten yourself on the other side—I'm going to drop heavy buckets in there with you and you can climb on them to get out."

I put my jacket on all the way and make sure the necklace is tight in my grip. In no time, I'm up on the grass with Gershom and Sandy. I throw my arms around my brother and whisper in his ear,

"It's your turn to get rescued. Don't forget!"

Gershom nods, his face thoughtful. He tells me where the paint cans came from, and I get chills knowing that God knocked those cans off that truck just for me.

"Well, let's eat. I'm starving." Gershom picks up the spilled burgers and we chow down. Cold hamburger for breakfast isn't the best, but it beats a stale, crusty roll. After we finish, we climb on our bikes and take off down the road. Neither of us says much; I am thinking about God and His love for me, and I hope Gershom is thinking about his need for rescue. The day passes quickly and before we know it, we are almost through Virginia—one more day closer to our mother and Alabama.

13 — Newman's Corner, NY

Hannah bustled into her office. It was a brand-new work week, and already she had a list of things to do as long as her arm. She gently set her laptop and purse on her desk and plopped into her chair. "No time to waste," she told herself.

She picked up the phone to call Justin's new foster mom. The emergency home they had placed him in Friday afternoon would have to do for another couple of days, and Hannah needed to make sure that would not upset anyone's plans. She was planning to call Officer Beech again, but something Justin's foster mom said prompted her to add another, more pressing item to her list.

As the morning went on, Hannah worked on securing Justin's future, filing paperwork for a sibling group to be formally adopted, and reviewing the cases of four other runaways. That list now held the names of six foster kids who were missing, but only one was of real concern to Hannah—two were nineteen, and three were older than ten and likely headed to family members. Those types of cases were never cause for too great of concern for most social workers, and so they weren't for Hannah, either. It was the two-year-old who went missing from day care that consumed Hannah's thoughts.

Hannah came back from lunch to find a pink note on her desk. She examined the note and read the fancy cursive: *I stopped by to ask you about Jasmine. I thought a personal visit might generate more concern on your part. We miss our girl and would rest easier knowing she was safe.* It was signed, *George and Stacy Whitman.*

Hannah moaned as she pulled up Stacy's phone number. On the second ring, Stacy answered.

"Hello? Miss Summers? Thank you for getting back to me. Do you have any word on Jasmine?" Stacy sounded breathless, with hope infused into every word.

Hannah took a deep breath. "Hi, Mrs. Whitman. I meant to call you earlier, but I just got so caught up in my other work. I do apologize." Hannah pulled out her notebook where she had taken notes from an earlier conversation.

Stacy burst out, "Is Jasmine okay? Do you know where she is? I just don't understand why she would run away like this.

George and I were so good to her. You know we were even discussing the possibility of adopting her. I just don't understand!"

Hannah shook her head. The Whitmans were wonderful people and great foster parents, but they were clueless when it came to legal proceedings and even the permanency of adoption. Hannah decided not to focus on that right now, but she flipped her notebook over and jotted down *Whitmans— adopting Jasmine?* so she could think about it later.

"Mrs. Whitman, I called the police on Friday, and I have a note here to follow up with them as soon as we get off here. On Friday after your first call, I did a little investigating, and this morning I visited their school. I questioned several of Gershom and Jasmine's classmates, and it turns out two of them sold their bikes to the kids at lunch on Friday."

Stacy was silent for a moment, then she asked, "Jasmine rides our daughter's old bike. Why would she get another one?"

"Well," Hannah was reluctant to tell Stacy her theory, but maybe it would ease the Whitmans' minds. "I think Jasmine and her brother are headed to Alabama in search of their birth mother."

"What! How did they know she was in Alabama, and why now, of all times, would they take off after her?" Stacy's hope seemed gone, replaced instead by indignation. "Have we not been good enough parents to Jasmine that she thought she had to travel a thousand miles to find someone better—someone she's never even met!"

Hannah closed her eyes at Stacy's outburst. Stacy meant well most of the time, but she could be so naïve sometimes.

"Mrs. Whitman—Stacy—calm down. I have someone in Alabama where the kids are headed who can look after them until we can make arrangements to bring them back here. Meanwhile, keep Jasmine's room ready and give us a few days to get this all sorted out."

Stacy's sigh echoed across the phone. "You're right. Okay. I know the police are good at finding kids, but let me know the minute Jasmine gets back to town. Thank you, Miss Summers."

Hannah hung up her phone and blew a sigh of relief. She immediately looked up the number for Auburn University and dialed Jontray Greene's extension. His voicemail clicked on after five rings. Hannah weighed the pros and cons of leaving a message and eventually hung up before the beep. She would try back later. This message wasn't one to be left on someone's voicemail.

She then called Officer Beech again, finally catching him at his desk. The conversation was short, as he was about to head out in search of their missing two-year-old, but he took all the information Hannah had to share about Gershom and Jasmine. He promised to add them to the list of kids they would look for.

Just before leaving for the day, Hannah called Jontray Greene once more, but again the voicemail picked up. *Oh well*, thought Hannah. *I'll try again tomorrow*. But like most days, work piled up on Hannah, and she completely forgot about calling

Jontray back. Since she had admonished Stacy to give her a few days, she didn't even think about Jasmine and Gershom until Thursday, when two policemen showed up at her office.

14 — Gershom and the Grocery Store

"Gershom, I'm sorry I fell in that hole this morning. I realize it made us start out later than normal."

We were riding across a bridge that spanned a raging river that looked scary to fall into, but I chanced a glance at my sister and shook my head. "It's not like you fell in there on purpose or anything. I mean, you didn't, right?"

Jasmine laughed, but then her face got serious. "No, I didn't do it on purpose, but I think maybe God did it on purpose."

I opened my mouth to say something, but at the end of the bridge was a sign welcoming us to Clarksville, Virginia. The sign proclaimed it was the last real town before North Carolina. I checked my watch and decided we should stop here for the night.

"Jasmine, let's stop here tonight. Then we'll buy some food before starting out tomorrow. First thing after this town is North Carolina, and who knows if we'll have an opportunity to find breakfast at any point."

The next morning, foghorns woke us up. Jasmine smiled at me and asked, "Can I watch the boats for a few minutes?"

I nodded my head and she took off, leaving me to study the map. It looked like there was another town before the border, making me curious about Clarksville's claim to be the last town. I called to Jasmine and told her my plan.

"We'll go down this road until we find something, a restaurant or grocery store or something. It shouldn't take long."

"Okay. How much money do we have left?"

"Um, about ten bucks, which, considering everything, is pretty good. Paul's pizza and the fact that he bought us those burgers certainly helped."

We set off and soon rounded a corner where Food Lion came into view. I smiled at Jasmine, and we parked our bikes and Sandy outside. Jasmine made a bee line for the candy aisle, but I tugged her arm toward the bread aisle.

"Candy won't fill us up or give us strength to ride. We could buy a loaf of bread and a jar of jelly, what do you think?"

"I thought jelly had to stay in the fridge. Mrs. Whitman always got onto me when I'd accidentally leave it out on the counter." Jasmine picked up a bag of bagels with raisins. "These look good."

I thought for a minute. "Maybe. Let's see if we can find something better, but we need to head out soon. Maybe if we buy a small jar of jelly, we'll have sandwiches for breakfast, lunch, and supper, and that should use up most of the jelly. It'll be fine for one day."

Jasmine put the bagels back and selected a loaf of potato bread. She carefully counted the slices then held it up. "Better? I love potato bread! And there are enough slices in here to last a bunch of sandwiches."

"How much is it?" I checked the price. "As long as the jelly is cheap, that's fine. What flavor do you want?"

When we arrived at the condiment aisle, we were blown away with all the choices. Jasmine picked up blueberry, then set it down for apple, then exchanged that for peach. I skimmed the prices and picked up a jar of grape. Jasmine groaned and said, "Fine."

As we made our way back to the main aisle, the selections of honey caught my eye. "Hey, since the jelly was so cheap, you want to get some honey too? We can have jelly sandwiches today and honey sandwiches tomorrow."

"Sounds good." Jasmine chose a bear-shaped honey bottle and batted her soulful eyes at me.

I sighed. "Okay, but what are you going to do with that when the honey is gone?"

Jasmine shrugged. "I don't know. But it will be more fun to eat honey out of this bottle than any other kind of bottle."

I handed Jasmine the bread. "Hold this under your arm, but don't squish it. Now put the jelly in one hand and the honey in the other. There. I'm going to get my money out." I reached into my pocket and pulled out a handful of jelly packets. "Hey! Where did these come from?"

Jasmine laughed. "Oh, I forgot about those! When we were at McDonald's with Paul, I grabbed those from the counter while you and Paul were ordering the extra burgers. I saw them and figured they might come in handy one day. I must have put them in your jacket instead of mine. They were free, right? I didn't actually steal them, did I?"

"No, you didn't steal them. I don't know that the employees would have been very happy with you for taking so many, but there's no law against it. Well, let's put the jar of jelly back. These packets will do nicely. We'll still get the honey, but this way we can also get a jar of nuts to snack on. Good protein, you know."

Jasmine just shrugged. I guess this was one of those things that I found fascinating but other kids didn't. I took a deep breath to steady myself. No need to go into a huge discussion about the importance of protein if Jasmine didn't care.

I put the jelly packets back in my pocket and counted out some money. After we paid for our food, we made our way back to our bikes.

"Oh no!" Jasmine yelled.

"What's the matter?" I asked as I set the bag of food in her bike basket.

"Sandy's gone! Where's my puppy?"

We looked all around the bikes and called to him. Then something caught my eye. A dog that looked suspiciously like Sandy sat in a girl's lap, wagging his entire backside while she pet him. I pointed to the girl in the wheelchair.

"Oh, she looks like she's enjoying him." Jasmine sighed. "Should I go over there and tell her his name, at least?"

Sandy licked the girl's face and her laughter drifted to us, followed by her question.

"Can we keep him, Mom? He doesn't have a collar, so he probably doesn't belong to anyone. Please?"

We watched the girl's mom step out from behind their van. She smiled at her daughter and her voice carried to us, "I don't know, Anna. He looks awfully dirty. He's probably a stray or something. I'm worried about disease."

I glanced down at Jasmine to see her clench her hands in front of her. "Come on, Jaz. Let's go tell them about Sandy. He will be happier with them. They can feed him good food and buy him a collar and leash." I gave Jasmine a quick squeeze, and we wheeled our bikes across the parking lot.

"Hey," Jasmine greeted the girl in the chair.

"Hi," she said back. She sat up straighter and asked, "Oh, is this your dog? He sure is cute!"

I shook my head. "It's kind of a long story, but he's not really ours. He's not really *anyone's*! We have been taking care of him, but I needed someone, and now you look like you need someone."

Anna scratched behind Sandy's ears. "What's his name?"

Jasmine reached over to pet Sandy. "We don't know. I named him Sandy when we got him, but you can probably call him whatever you want. He's yours now if your mom says it's okay."

Anna looked up at her mom with pleading eyes. "Please, mom? He just needs a bath and he'll be as good as new! I know my birthday's not for two more weeks, but hey, this dog is free. Please?"

Anna's mom laughed. "You've convinced me! Let's get you two loaded up. I guess we need to stop by the pet store on our way home now."

Anna handed Sandy to her mom and turned toward us. "Thank you. You just made my birthday wish come true." Her eyes glistened and her smile lit up her entire face. I mumbled "You're welcome," and headed back to my bike. Jasmine gave Anna a quick wave and followed me.

When we got back to our bikes, I heard Jasmine sniff.

"I'll miss Sandy," she quietly announced.

"Yeah, me too," I agreed. "But it's better this way. For all of us, you know?"

Jasmine nodded. She felt for her cross necklace and whispered, "God is looking out for Sandy, too, and knows he will be better with that family. Let's go, Gersh." I nodded my agreement, and after a quick look at the map, we headed south.

That other town that was on the map didn't even have a red light. I supposed that was what Clarksville meant by being the last "real" town.

Neither of us said anything until we crossed the North Carolina border, at which point we stopped for a quick break. Then it was back on the bikes to get about halfway through North Carolina before stopping for the night. I was glad nothing major happened on the road today, because losing Sandy was surely enough excitement for one day.

15 — Jasmine's Testimony

All day long I think about Sandy. Yesterday, we left him with a girl who obviously needs him more than I do, especially since God rescued me from myself, and I can feel His love inside my heart. As we ride today, I also think about the ways God has protected us and taken care of us on this journey. We were crazy to do this, but I have learned so much already, about myself and Gershom and God.

Gershom doesn't seem interested in having God rescue him. Maybe if I tell him about what happened to me, he might change his mind.

"Hey, Gersh, can I talk to you for a minute?" I pedal up next to him, and we ride side-by-side for a ways. Even though it's a weekday, not many cars are on this particular stretch of highway.

"You can always talk to me about stuff, Jaz. What's on your mind?"

"I want to tell you about what happened in my heart when God rescued me. Every time I bring it up you always change the subject, but I really want to talk to you about this. Is that okay?"

Gershom's jaw clenches several times, but then he blows out his breath and says, "Okay. I promise I won't change the subject this time. Now, what is it you want to tell me?"

I smile and steer with one hand so I can hold my necklace in the other. "First, I realized that I couldn't live my life by myself, with no help. I know you've done a good job protecting me, but I think it was really God protecting me this whole time, and He was just using you. That time those girls attacked me on the bus when I wore my big red bow? And that time I fell and twisted my ankle in gym class? Even recently, when Paul would have run me over if you hadn't made me get out of the road—all those times, God was protecting me."

Gershom nods. Now that he promised to listen, I think he is actually *listening*. I continue.

"Next came the easy part. Once I realized I needed God's help in my life, I just asked him, and He put His hand on my heart and I can feel Him, in here." I lay my hand over my heart and smile. "And that's all you need to do, too. Just tell him that you know you can't do it by yourself, and ask God to help you."

"Hm, I guess that makes sense," Gershom says. "But what if I don't think I need God's help? I feel like my life is fine just the way it is."

"Really?" I slant my eyes at Gershom. "Then why are we on this cross-country trip in search of people we've never met in the hopes that they can be part of our lives to enrich our very souls?" By the end, my voice is screeching, and I'm out of breath.

Gershom tips his head. "You know that we have both met our mother at some point in our past. I mean, we didn't go into foster care the second we were born. And I'm not searching for anyone to enrich my very soul. You're so melodramatic."

"Yeah, I know. Mrs. Whitman called me that all the time." I wave away his words, still discouraged. "But you know what I mean. If you felt fine, we wouldn't be here, missing Sandy and eating jelly packets from McDonald's."

"I'm sorry, Jaz. I'm doing my best—"

"Hey, listen!" I interrupt Gershom. "Do you hear that?"

Beautiful singing wafts toward us on the breeze. The farther we pedal, the louder the music is, until finally we come to a T in the road and stop, facing a little white church. The front doors stand wide open, welcoming us in.

"Can we stay and listen to the music? Please, Gersh? I won't ask to stop again until we get to Alabama." I plead with my eyes until finally Gershom throws his hands up and walks his bike over to the front porch of the church.

"Stay quiet!" he whispers.

I nod my head, and we pull up to a section of grass underneath the first window and make ourselves comfortable. We barely get settled when the music stops. Gershom jumps up, but I pull on his leg, making him sit again.

"They might start again in a minute. Be patient!"

Gershom rolls his eyes, and we wait. Soon, a deep voice booms, "God loves you and wants to save you tonight!"

Gershom and I look at each other, our eyes as wide as could be. This guy sounds serious!

"You are living in sin, but God sent His Son to die for you so you don't have to go to Hell. Won't you tell Him you're sorry for your sin and accept His free gift of salvation? Won't you secure a home in Heaven tonight? It's as easy as that!"

Gershom leans over and whispers in my ear, "That's not what you said I had to do."

I shrug. "I'm not an expert. Maybe we should go in there and ask and they can clarify things for us."

"Maybe we shouldn't! Like I said, my life is fine." But Gershom's face pales at the preacher's next words.

"This world was not made for us. We should be strangers in this land, just like Moses and his son Gershom were in the wilderness. But if you're like Moses, you'll allow your sin to separate you from God. Be a Gershom; enter the Promised Land!"

At that, my brother springs up from beside me and stomps over to his bike. His wags his finger at me and says, "I am Gershom. I'm already Gershom. I don't need to be saved from Hell to be myself! That's a crazy person in there. He should be locked up in the loony bin!"

I run over to Gershom and shush him. "Not so loud—they're going to hear you! Come on, let's just forget about him and keep going, okay? I'm sorry I made us stop."

I follow Gershom farther away from the church and the strange message. Maybe one day someone can explain it all to us and we can both find peace, but first I figure we should concentrate on getting to Alabama in one piece without fighting anymore.

16 — Gershom's Cold-Blooded Encounter

Another day, brand new with possibilities. I spread my map out on the ground and figured that since we were almost to South Carolina now, we could probably get two-thirds of the way through that state today.

I nudged Jasmine's leg. She rolled over and groaned, "Is it morning already? Why does the sun have to come up so early every single day?"

"Come on, Jaz. Let's go to South Carolina. We've already experienced so much on this trip; do you think we can make it through even one day without a big catastrophe?"

"Hmm." Jasmine opened a jelly packet and smeared it across one piece of bread. I decided to go with a honey sandwich for breakfast. We made quick work of our food and packed up for another day on the road. Ever since Sandy found a new home and wasn't occupying Jasmine's basket anymore, she carried her backpack there.

Ten minutes down the road, we came to a nice-looking town. Across the first intersection was a banner proclaiming "Cold-Blooded Encounters Visits Monroe, NC!" I shuddered. I didn't like cold-blooded anything, and I certainly didn't want to encounter one.

"Jaz, let's get through this town quickly. It looks like they have snakes and stuff."

"Ew! Now I'm glad I don't have Sandy anymore. Those big snakes like to eat little puppies, did you know that?" Jasmine pedaled past me and called for me to hurry.

By the time we got to the second intersection, it appeared that every person in this town had turned out for this display of creatures. Cars were parked up and down both sides of the street, and the sidewalks were packed. We got off our bikes and had to walk toward the next intersection. A kid passed us on his scooter and turned to point and laugh at my pink bicycle. I just rolled my eyes.

We saw several more banners, each claiming something more amazing than the last. When we got to a banner that read "Esmeralda Eats Jacob Whole!", I knew that as gruesome as that sounded, we had to stop and find out what was going on.

A girl with braids walked past, and Jasmine tapped her on the shoulder to get her attention. "Hey, who are Esmeralda and Jacob?" she asked.

The girl stopped and answered, "Esmeralda is a boa constrictor. Jacob is a pig that has Dipped Shoulder, also known as Humpy Back." She took a step away from us and seemed to ignore us.

Jasmine looked at me and asked, "What's Humpy Back?"

I shrugged. "I don't know any more than you do. You've never read about it in any of your doctor books?"

"The animals I concentrate on are common pets. Pigs aren't really that popular when it comes to pets." Jasmine tapped the girl on the shoulder again. "Excuse me? What is Humpy Back?"

The girl's braids flew straight out when she turned around to face us. With an exasperated sigh, she said, "It's when the back half of the pig dips down, and the front half humps over. Jacob's case is extreme, and he's almost paralyzed. You do know what being paralyzed means, right?"

Jasmine snorted. "I'm from New York; I'm not stupid."

The girl held out her arms. "Well, you never know around here. Since there's no cure for Jacob, my dad sold him to Cold-Blooded Encounters for them to feed to their biggest snake. This event has only been in the news all week. Where have you been?"

A cheer rose from the crowd, and everyone automatically pressed in closer. There was a stage set up in the middle of the street where two huge terrariums sat side by side, with the biggest snake I'd ever seen in one of them. I bent down and asked Jasmine if she could see.

"Yeah," she whispered, "but I don't know if I want to look or not!"

A big burly man in overalls and a plaid shirt hefted a funny-looking pig high in the air. A man in a suit stood nearby with a megaphone pressed against his lips. The megaphone screeched when he depressed the talk button.

"Attention: Everyone! Keith is lowering Jacob into Esmeralda's tank now! She hasn't been fed in three weeks so she should be quite hungry."

The man suspended his speech as Keith set the pig in the tank. Keith backed up a step to admire his handiwork. The man in the suit resumed his play-by-play commentary.

"And now Keith is removing the dividing plate between the two tanks. Wow! Folks, I sure hope you can see this! Esmeralda is making a beeline for that pig! Look at that snake go, would ya!"

Cheers rang out throughout the crowd. The sentiment shared by most seemed to be that of joy and wonder; however, I felt sick, and by the greenish tint to Jasmine's face, I gathered that she did, too. I grabbed her elbow and steered her toward the edge of the crowd. A breath of fresh air hit us in the face, and after a couple deep gulps, I felt better.

"Whew, I think—I think I don't ever want to see that again," Jasmine said.

I whole-heartedly agreed with her. "Let's get out of here before someone starts asking us questions. We seem to be the only ones here not immensely enjoying ourselves."

Outside of the crowd, we hopped on our bikes and pedaled down the street. When we got to the intersection where we had to turn to stay heading south, I stopped and looked back. There were so many people, out with their families, enjoying themselves on a warm Thursday morning. I felt a twinge of something in my gut. I wanted my own family with whom to watch creatures eating other creatures, disgusting though it was.

I quickly caught up with Jasmine and listened while she replayed the morning's adventures from every angle. I was relieved when we made it halfway through South Carolina without encounters of any other kind. I just wanted to get to where we were going, and soon. Jasmine was great, and I was okay if she ended up being my only family, but I couldn't help but think how nice it would be to have actual parents.

17 — Newman's Corner, NY

Thursday morning dawned bright and clear, starting just the way Hannah loved. She stood at her car for a minute, letting the sun bathe her cheeks before bustling into her office, waving a hello to Patricia on her way past.

"Ah, another beautiful day, Daisy," Hannah told her plant. She'd realized earlier in the week that carrying on a conversation, one-sided though it may be, helped her think through her problems, so she'd brought one of her spider plants from home to her office. Already, she had unraveled several mysteries this week.

The day offered a myriad of challenges that only a social worker could navigate, and before Hannah knew it, there was only one more hour before she left for the day. As she wrapped up her day's activities, her desk phone buzzed, letting her know it was Pat from the front office. "Hey Pat, what's up?"

"Uh, Hannah, there are two officers on their way to your office!" Pat sounded distressed, but policemen often came around the Office of Children and Family Services.

"Thanks for the heads-up! I'm sure everything is fine. Thursday is my usual debriefing day with the police, remember? I'm actually surprised they didn't come this morning." A knock sounded on Hannah's door, and she whispered into the phone, "Gotta go." Loudly, she called, "Come in!"

"Hannah Summers?" The tall policeman removed his hat and twisted it in his hands.

"Yes, what can I help you with today, Officer? Please, come in and have a seat." Hannah stood up and gestured toward her two plush chairs that faced her desk. "I haven't seen you around here before. Are you new to the area?"

The shorter policeman removed his hat before he spoke. "Actually, yes we are, ma'am. I am Officer Beech, just transferred from homicide over in Pennsylvania, and this is Officer Ginger, just graduated from the academy. You are the social worker for Jasmine Yanez, correct?"

"Oh, Officer Beech! Nice to meet you in person. Yes, have you been able to find out anything about Jasmine? And her brother, Gershom? He'll be thirteen in a few weeks, and he's always struck me as an old soul, you know? But I do worry about him. He'd only just begun to deal with how to avoid meltdowns in therapy."

Officer Beech shook his head. "We've been so consumed this week with finding that missing toddler. We were in constant contact with your boss, I think."

"Oh yes," Hannah agreed. "When the missing child is of such tender age, Allen Rock handles the case. I heard she was found this morning?"

"Yes, thankfully. An aunt had snatched her from daycare. Now, about Jasmine?"

Hannah held up one finger. "I have a phone number here somewhere." She spun around to dig in the kids' file. "Ah, here it is. Jontray Greene. I'm honestly not entirely sure how he's related to the kids, as the social worker who brought the kids in had written his name in their file, with a note attached saying 'Do not contact unless an emergency.' Well, I think this counts as an emergency!"

Officer Ginger took the paper and stuck it in the file they had brought with them.

She was reluctant to admit that she had never gotten through to that relative and that he had no idea two children were headed his way, although she did reassure the policemen that she had already called twice since last Friday.

She cleared her throat and continued, "Now if you kind gentlemen would excuse me, I have other children that I need to see to the needs of. Your office will be the first one I call when the Alabama relative makes contact to say the children have arrived."

She raised an eyebrow, and Officer Beech hurried to say, "Oh yes, and you'll be our first call when we find out anything, also."

The two policemen each nodded at Hannah, replaced their hats, and made their way out to their squad car. Now that the two-year-old had been found, they were able to devote more time to the older kids. Once they arrived at the station, they scanned Stacy Whitman's photo of Gershom and Jasmine into the computer. By this time tomorrow, the entire East Coast would know who the Yanez kids were, and they were convinced that it would just be a matter of time before someone called in to report a sighting.

18 — Gershom's TV Appearance

"Jaz, I've been thinking about something." I stretched and sat up. Jasmine handed me two pieces of bread and offered me the honey and a jelly packet. I took the honey and shook my head, letting her know she could have the jelly.

"Do I want to know?" Jasmine quirked an eyebrow at me before smearing jelly on her bread. She carefully placed the used jelly packet in our trash bag from Food Lion.

"Very funny. I've been thinking that we've stayed on the main roads this whole trip, and no one has recognized us or anything. Don't you think that's a little suspicious?" I broke my crust off for Sandy before remembering that he was several states away.

"I guess," Jasmine said thoughtfully. "Maybe it's just God keeping us safe and allowing us to get to Auburn. Maybe He knows there is something or someone there that we need."

"Hmm." Ever since Jasmine told me that God rescued her from herself, she managed to insert Him into just about every conversation. I didn't really mind, but He was definitely not the first thing I thought of when I tried to think up reasons for stuff happening.

"Well, today I think we should cross Georgia on back roads. It shouldn't really take too much longer, and anyway, it won't do us any good to get to the University before Monday. Are you about ready to go?" I stood up and brushed the breadcrumbs from my clothes. I had always been conscious of how I presented myself and tried to be decently clean, so this trip was making me miserable. When we finally got to where we were going, I would be glad to do some laundry, take a nice long shower, and get a haircut for my wild, out-of-control mop.

We started the morning on the main road. I needed a better map to plan back roads, and I kept my eye out for a gas station. Clouds were thick overhead, making the air feel muggy. Not long after I noticed the humid weather, Jasmine commented about the same thing.

"If I lick the air, I almost have to swallow because of all the water in the air."

It was too hot to answer, so I nodded. We continued in silence for several hours until a truck stop came into view. I pointed at it and veered that direction.

"Bathroom break. I'm going to look for a map of just Georgia so I can figure out back roads to Alabama. We have a little money left and our water bottles have walked their last leg, I'm afraid. Can you find some water while I look for the map?"

"Okay," Jasmine said. "I wish I had a hat to keep this heat off. Plus, it could shield my face from anyone too curious."

"Sorry, Jaz, we don't have *that* much money left over." She smiled at me, but I felt like a lowlife—not being able to provide basic needs for my sister.

As I handed the cashier the rest of my bills to pay for the map and water, I heard my name, but it wasn't Jasmine calling me. I spun around and spotted the TV in the corner. The lady sounded so sincere in her plea:

"The number is displayed on the screen. The children's names once again are Gershom and Jasmine Yanez. Jasmine's mom is distraught and urges anyone who may see these children to please call the police. You could be instrumental in bringing this family back together."

Jasmine jumped up next to me and squeezed my arm. Before she had a chance to say anything, I snatched my bag of purchases from the cashier's outstretched hand, shushed her, and dragged her outside. Once we were back on our bikes headed in the general direction of south-west, I blurted out the only thing that came to mind.

"When was that picture of us taken? It's a horrible picture!"

For some reason, Jasmine thought that was hilarious. "That picture was taken a couple years ago before my school play in second grade, remember? It's kinda sad that the only picture they had of us was from three years ago."

"Well, that could be a good thing. We look so different now than we did at seven and nine. Maybe no one in there recognized us, but it's a good thing I already decided to take the back roads. Do you think you should revisit your theory that it was God Who kept people from recognizing us?"

Jasmine sniffed. "And Who do you think it was that made sure we were in that particular gas station when that particular TV aired that particular news story? I don't think it was a coincidence."

I hadn't considered that. "You always have an answer for everything, don't you?"

"But they're good answers, right?"

"Yeah, okay. We should stop soon for lunch. It will give me a chance to map out the rest of our trip." We passed a bridge, and we both gravitated toward it.

"Shade!" Jasmine shouted. I laughed. Shade was always a good thing in this weather, but with so many clouds, it didn't make much of a difference under the bridge.

When I removed the bag of food from Jasmine's backpack, I noticed small black dots moving all over the contents inside. When I opened the bag and peered inside, I discovered ants—hundreds and thousands and maybe even millions of ants, quickly dissecting our bread and trying to make off with our honey.

"Gross!" Jasmine squealed. "Can you get them all off? That is so disgusting, Gersh! Ew!"

"Okay, okay! Surely it's not as bad as Esmeralda eating Jacob whole, is it?" I shook the bag, trying to dislodge the ants, but to no avail.

Jasmine calmed down at the mention of the snake. "No," she conceded, "I don't think anything is worse than that." She shuddered and took a deep breath.

"Jaz, there's no way I can get rid of all these ants. Do you want to just eat them with our sandwich? I mean, I think people in certain parts of Africa do it all the time." The thought *was* a little disturbing since we weren't in Africa.

"Gershom! No way. Just because they do it doesn't mean I need to. I'm gonna have to be a lot hungrier than this before I eat bugs." Jasmine turned her back to me and harrumphed.

"If we wait until I get all the ants out of here, the next meal we'll be eating will be supper tomorrow, just so you know." I dumped everything out of the bag and two jelly packets tumbled out. I threw them both to her and said, "At least you can eat this. No ants, I promise."

I stared down at the bread and honey crawling with ants, and my stomach turned. I just couldn't bring myself to ingest the tiny creatures, either. I glanced around, hoping for a miracle. Just as I was going to admit defeat, a flash of red caught my eye.

"Hey, Jaz, stay right here. I think I see something over there. I'll be right back." As I made my way across the expanse of rocks to the other side of the bridge, I heard Jasmine declare,

"Thank you, God, for this jelly. Please let it fill my tummy. And if not, please let Gershom find more food, even though he doesn't quite trust You yet. The End."

I snorted. In all my life, I'd never heard a prayer close like that. Of course, I hadn't heard many prayers at all, but I was pretty sure there were holier words than "the end" you were supposed to say. When I reached the spot where I thought I had seen something, I stopped. There was nothing here except for more rocks; however, when I bent down to get a closer look, I saw three packages of peanut butter crackers, just lying on the ground.

I turned a complete circle, looking for whoever had left the food. I even called out, just to be certain. "Hello? Anyone here? You left something behind!"

When there was no answer, I picked up the packages and headed back toward Jasmine. I held out one package to her and said, "Here. God answered your prayer. I found this over there. Not opened, no bugs. There were two more packages, and I'll split one of them with you."

Jasmine didn't say anything, just raised her eyebrows at me. I sat down and mumbled, "Thank you God for this food," before tearing into my crackers.

When she was finished with her lunch, Jasmine looked again with dismay at the bread and honey. "I guess it's okay. There were only three pieces of bread left, anyway. This way we won't fight over who gets the last piece."

"Maybe after a while the ants will crawl away," I suggested.

"Maybe we should leave the bread here. Whoever left those crackers for us might not mind eating bugs. But Gersh," Jasmine turned to me, "what are we going to do about supper tonight, and all our meals tomorrow, and the next day, and the next?" Two tears slid down her face, making clear tracks.

As much as I didn't want to admit it, I realized I needed to remind Jasmine of her faith. "Just a minute ago, you prayed that I'd find food—and I did. Don't you think God can take care of the rest of our meals until we get to Auburn?"

Jasmine sniffed and wiped her cheeks with her jacket sleeve. It was not any cleaner than anything else and she just made a mess of her face, but her smile shone brightly through the smeared dirt. "Of course, you're right! God is watching out for us and He will provide for us. Maybe next time I should pray for milkshakes and chicken fingers."

I smiled. “You do that. Who knows, maybe we can find a restaurant as they’re closing and get them to give us their leftovers.”

As Jasmine and I rode, we discussed which restaurants we should keep an eye out for. When supper time rolled around, we had worked ourselves up quite the appetite. I was about to break it to Jasmine that we had no food and no money and were going to go hungry tonight when we passed a family setting up their yard for a yard sale the next day. A sign stood prominently by the road, “*Free chicken fingers to anyone who wants to help*.”

Without saying a word, we braked and immediately set to work helping the family lay out their possessions. I heard a sniff and glanced at Jasmine. She was mumbling something, with tears making fresh streaks down her face.

“Jaz, what’s wrong?” I whispered the next time I passed her.

“Chicken fingers, Gershom! It’s exactly what I prayed for! I don’t know what else God has to do to convince you He’s watching out for us.”

I shook my head, not out of denial, but because my sister’s heart was so tender. Her tears moved me, and I tucked this night away so later, I could more closely examine my ever-changing feelings about God.

After a few minutes, a man on crutches came outside to supervise. He waved at us and called us over.

"What are y'all doing here? Shouldn't y'all be at home?"

I set down the rolled-up rug I was carrying and squared my shoulders. "We're just looking for ways to help out around the community, sir." Listen to me, being all civic-minded.

Jasmine piped up next to me, "We sure wouldn't mind some of those chicken fingers you promised on your sign, there, either."

The man grunted and used his crutch to point to the other side of the yard. "All righty, then. Put that over yonder. I reckon we're about done here. Let me go git yer grub."

After the man disappeared back inside, Jasmine poked me in the ribs. "I don't want grub. I want chicken fingers." She made a face. "Grub sounds gross."

I shook my head. "I think grub is just his word for food. I think he's going to bring out chicken fingers. Did you hear all his other funny words? And his accent? No question we're in the South!"

Sure enough, a minute later the man and a lady came out with a plastic bowl filled with chicken fingers. When I noticed they had given us plenty of extra for the road, I knew God really was watching out for us.

19 — Jasmine's New Friends

"Hey, look!" Gershom calls to me. I let out a yell as we pass the sign: *Keep Alabama the Beautiful*.

"We're almost there! We're almost to Jontray Greene!" I pedal up to Gershom and he laughs when he sees me bouncing on my bike.

"Calm down, there! We don't even know if he can help us find our mother. Don't get your hopes up too high."

I nod, but butterflies take up residence in my belly. I think it's too late for that. After so many days on the road with adventures, the entire day yesterday passed as boring as could be. Of course, when we ate our leftover chicken, I couldn't help but tease Gershom about there not being any milkshakes. He was quiet about it, so I just talked to God in my head, asking Him to show Gershom how important it is that he let God rescue him.

A couple hours pass, and after I finally manage to get my mind on something other than Jontray Greene and my mother, we pass another sign, this one declaring a town called Opelika.

"Sounds like an animal," I tell Gershom. "Like a mixed-up Okapi."

He nods. "Let's pull over for a minute. I need to check the map. I think we're pretty close to Auburn, but everything will be closed tonight. We can spend the night here—our last night on the road—and get to the University first thing tomorrow morning."

"Okay. I'm hungry anyway. Too bad there aren't food places on that map." I look around, hoping to spot a restaurant.

"Jasmine, do you smell that? Take a whiff!" Gershom takes a deep breath and looks around too, searching for the origin of the aroma.

"Mmm. Smells like pork and chicken and sauce and hot dogs and I don't know what else but it's good!" I spot a plume of smoke about three streets over and point it out to Gershom. "Look! Let's find it. Maybe it's a cookout. Do you think if they have extra, they won't mind sharing?"

In no time, we pull into a small parking lot. There is a church sign by the road and on the sidewalk are two huge black stoves with smoke billowing out the tops. A man with an orange and blue apron is directing traffic with his barbeque fork.

"Well, hello there." A lady holding a baby walks up to us and invites us to join them for supper. "We have plenty. I'll set you up at the kids' table over here. Come on! Now do either of you like okra or collard greens?"

"Um," I swallow hard. Neither of those sounds very appetizing.

"Just some chicken is fine, thank you." I look at Gershom and tell him *thank you* with my eyes.

"All right, well, here you go. This is Ronnie, Grace, Maybelle, and Sarah. Kids, make the newcomers feel welcome." The nice lady turns to me and says, "If you need anything, I'll be with my husband by the barbeque pits, okay?" When I nod, the lady turns and walks away.

I grab Gershom's hand. The four kids the lady introduced us to are staring at us. Ronnie holds out his hand to Gershom.

"Nice to meet you. What's your name? Please, sit." He motions to the empty seats around him.

Gershom sits across from Ronnie after shaking his hand, and I sit next to Gershom, putting Grace on my other side and Maybelle across from me.

"I'm Gershom, this is Jasmine. We, uh, smelled the smoke and thought we'd check it out."

I smile. Way to keep it simple and truthful.

We pick up our forks, but the chicken is stringy and covered in sauce. The bread is the biggest roll I have ever seen.

"Do it like this." Grace shows me her chicken sandwich. "Isn't it yummy? My daddy makes the best smoked barbeque."

Maybelle nods her agreement. I smile at them and try a bite. It is rather good. The food on my plate fills me up, and I enjoy a conversation with Grace and Maybelle. They're close to my age, and we have lots to talk about. Gershom gets another helping, and when he finishes, he nudges me.

"It's time to go, little sister," he whispers.

I turn and scowl at him. "I made new friends. I don't want to leave yet."

Gershom lays his hand on my shoulder. "If they find out we're runaways, not kids down the street who just moved in, they'll call the police. We are so close, Jaz. We can't risk it. Maybe after we meet Jontray and find our mother we can come back here and you can play with your new friends. But for now, let's go."

His eyes plead with mine, and I try not to look because I know I'll give in. "Oh fine. But let's at least get some rolls to take with us for breakfast tomorrow."

"I already got some, see?" Gershom shows me his backpack.

I cross my arms and hiss at him, "Well, I'm not happy about it."

"Yeah, you've made that clear. Now come on, before that lady notices we're leaving and tries to stop us."

We wave goodbye to our new friends, with promises that we will come visit again soon. As much as I am disinclined to admit it, I know Gershom is right. We need to concentrate on finding our mother. Strangers, no matter how nice, will have to wait.

20 — Opelika, AL

"Well, Preacher, that was a mighty fine barbeque, if I do say so myself." Jon patted the pastor's back. "We should do this more often."

Pastor Mike nodded his head. "It was good to see so many visitors. Were many of them from the school?"

Jon shrugged. "I invited a bunch, but I only saw two familiar faces. Other members must have had successful invites, too."

Jon's wife appeared from inside the building and announced, "Everything's cleaned up in there. Time to go home now?"

Jon nodded and looked at the pastor. "Everything's pretty much cleaned up out here, too."

Pastor Mike took the baby from his wife and said, "Corral the children, honey. Time to go."

As the kids piled into their van, Jon overheard them talking about two new kids that ate supper with them.

"Gershom's a couple years younger than I am," declared Ronnie. "But he seemed pretty cool. Can you imagine what it must have been like growing up in New York? Getting snow every single winter and—" the van door slammed shut on the rest of his sentence.

Jon helped his wife into their car, thoughtful about those two kids. Halfway home, he said to Karis, "Did you see those two kids sitting with Pastor Mike's kids?"

Karis thought back for a minute and said, "No, whose were they?"

Jon clucked his tongue. "Not sure. The girl looked like the spitting image of my sister, though. How is that even possible? Stephanie doesn't have kids."

"I have no idea. You're sure, though? I mean, I know she never talked about having kids, but we don't know what really happened for those three years she lived in New York. Is it possible?"

Jon shook his head. "No way. Having kids is a major thing. You'd tell your family, even if they didn't like you very much."

Karis shrugged in the dark. "Maybe. But you and your father were so angry at her for running away with Kasper. Maybe she wouldn't tell you out of spite?"

"Hm. I just can't believe my own sister would have kids and not tell us. And I really can't believe she would have kids and then leave them halfway across the country without telling us." Jon hit the steering wheel and tried to shake the image of Jasmine's gray-blue eyes.

Karis reached across the car to rub Jon's shoulder. "Tomorrow after classes, would you like to go visit your sister? You can swing by and pick me up—I should be finished at the high school by 2:15."

Jon let that idea mull in his brain. For the rest of the drive home, he prayed about the benefits of visiting Stephanie. As they pulled into their driveway, he told his wife, "Yes, that's a good plan. I haven't been by to see her in a couple days. A visit will surely dispel these crazy thoughts. Thanks, Karis."

Jon smiled as he realized that by tomorrow, he could put this whole thing behind him. He would've spent many more moments in earnest prayer if he'd known that tomorrow would bring a lot more than just a casual visit with his sister.

21 — Gershom and the Professor

"Wow," Jasmine breathed out next to me. "This place is huge!"

We stopped our bikes at the campus gate and took in the site. Buildings rose into the sky multiple stories high in every direction we looked, and we could see the road wind around to more buildings further away.

Jasmine voiced the question burning in my mind. "How are we going to find Jontray Greene?"

"Um, well, maybe there's an information desk inside one of these buildings." I looked around for a place to park our bikes. "Here, Jaz, let's leave our bikes here with these others. They should be fine for a few minutes."

After stowing our bikes, which stand out among the others like the outsiders we are, we walked into the first building we came to. There were people milling about everywhere. A little desk sat off to one side, so I grabbed Jasmine's hand and pulled her toward the desk.

"Excuse me," I said to the lady behind the desk.

"Yes?" She looked surprised to see us and I wondered if we were even close to being in the right place.

"We're looking for a man named Jontray Greene. He's probably a professor. Do you know him, and where we could find him?"

"Honey, you're on the wrong end of campus. This here's a dorm, where all the students live. Here," she whipped out a pamphlet that folded out to show a map of Auburn University. "You're here—" she circled a long house with her sparkly green pen, "—and you want to go here." She drew a route from the house to a building on the other side of the map, then circled that building. "Professor Greene teaches in here. His office is on the third floor."

"Thanks a lot." I told her and studied the map for a minute. "Come on Jaz, let's go."

We made our way back to our bikes and headed across campus. My mind was spinning the entire time. How was Jontray Greene related to us? Would he be happy to see us? So many questions, and now that we were almost there, my nerves intensified. I took a deep breath, trying to ground myself. In a few short minutes, we would know if this trip was worth all the trouble we'd been through in the past two weeks.

"Well, here we are. Moment of truth," I said to Jasmine as we parked our bikes at another bike rack. "Let's go!"

We found a staircase off to one side of a big lobby and climbed to the third floor. In front of the staircase landing was a handy plaque, indicating the different directions of the offices for the various professors who taught in this building.

"Jontray Greene, to the left." Jasmine slinked behind me, like she was afraid someone would catch us sneaking around and throw us out. I knew exactly how she felt. We finally made it to the correct door, and I raised my hand to knock, but the door swung open and a big man almost ran into me.

"Oh, I'm sorry there, son. Didn't see you—hey, weren't you at Heritage Baptist Church last night? The barbeque?" He stared intently at Jasmine like she had three heads.

I felt her clasp my hand and I squeezed, offering her some assurance. She squeezed back, giving me some, too. "Yes, sir, we were there."

"Well, what can I do for y'all?" He shook his head and moved his gaze to me.

"We're looking for Jontray Greene. Do you know him?" I asked, hoping that I looked braver than I felt.

"I'm Professor Greene."

"Oh." Suddenly, my mouth went dry and my palms started to sweat. All sane thoughts fled my mind.

The Professor must have noticed my anxiety, because he said, "Why don't you come in and sit down. I have a few minutes before my first class starts. There you go. Now, let's start with your names."

Jasmine and I plopped down on the little couch in the Professor's office. The sticky feel of the plastic jolted my mind back into high gear. After explaining who we were, where we were from, and why we had come, the Professor sat back in his chair, his face somber. He rubbed his face with his hands and repeated over and over,

"How could I have known?"

I looked at Jasmine, and we shrugged at each other. Jasmine offered to get him some water, although I didn't think she even knew where any water was.

"No, no, I'm fine. I just need to—process." The Professor sat back and stared at us.

Jasmine squirmed in her seat. I thought maybe we should go, but he still hadn't said anything about our mother, and I was staying put until he gave us some information.

"Excuse me, I know this is a lot to throw at a person all at once, but do you know our mother, Stephanie Yanez?"

At the mention of our mother's name, the Professor snapped to attention. He came around his desk and leaned up against it. "Yes, I know your mother. Stephanie is my sister. She lives in a facility not far from here. I was actually going to visit her this afternoon, but now I'm not so sure that's a good idea."

My mind raced. "What do you mean, she lives in a facility? Like, a hospital?"

And then something dawned on me. "Wait, so that means that you're our uncle, doesn't it? We have an uncle, Jaz!"

The Professor rubbed his face again. "Wow, yeah, I guess I would be your Uncle Jontray. Or just Uncle Jon. Most people just call me Jon, except for Stephanie. She was always a stickler on the full name thing."

He reached around his desk for a picture frame. He handed it to Jasmine and said, "This is your mother. You have her eyes. Those same gray-blue eyes she would turn on me when we were kids any time she wanted her way."

I leaned over and studied the picture in Jasmine's hands. The lady had dark skin, like us—like the professor—her shining smile radiating youth and happiness. She was seated in front of a tall man who had his hand on her shoulder. "Who is she with?" I asked.

"That would be your dad, Kasper Yanez. He was a firefighter in New York City."

I picked up on his use of the past tense. "What do you mean, he was? Where is he now?"

The Professor hesitated. “He was very brave; I want you to know that. When Stephanie first met him, our dad didn’t like him, and so naturally I didn’t, either. We said things we later regretted, but it was too late; we had driven Stephanie away. She left—moved to New York with Kasper—for three years. Then there was a terrible fire. A warehouse exploded and sent multiple buildings up in flames, including an apartment complex. Kasper—your dad—and several other firemen never made it out. They died saving people’s lives. Soon after the funeral, Stephanie moved back here.”

I looked at Jasmine. Tears streamed down her cheeks, cleaning away dirt and dust from our trip, and she hugged the picture of our parents to her chest.

After a minute, she handed me the picture frame and stood to hug our new Uncle Jon. She mumbled something into his shirt, and he pulled away to hear her better.

She repeated, “You didn’t know about us, did you?”

Uncle Jon knelt down next to Jasmine and reached out to grasp my hand. “If I had known about you, I would have brought you down here to live with me. I would never have left family alone. You believe me, don’t you?”

Jasmine nodded. I thought he was probably being sincere, too, since it looked like he was about to cry. I decided to take hold of the situation before either of us men started crying.

“So, can we visit our mom?”

Uncle Jon looked thoughtful. "Let me make some phone calls. I think we can work that out."

Jasmine and I glanced at each other. So much had already happened today, and now we were about to see our mother. As excited as I was, trepidation filled my heart to think of my mother in a facility. I knew I couldn't rest until I had seen for myself that she was okay.

22 — Jasmine and Aunt Karis

Uncle Jon is quick on the phone, even though he makes several calls. The police in New York don't sound too mad at us, judging from Uncle Jon's smile. He promised to call again tomorrow to get further instructions. And I could hear his wife's squeals from this side of the desk. After a few minutes, we all walk outside, and Gershom and I get on our bikes. When Uncle Jon sees us preparing to follow him, he says, "Let's put your bikes in the trunk of my car. That way you can ride with me."

I'm all for a different mode of transportation after all those hours on my bike, so we hop in his car and take off down the road. Our sweaty, dirty bodies fill the car with quite the unpleasant odor, and Uncle Jon cracks open all the windows.

"It's a beautiful day—why not enjoy the breeze?" he asks. I make a face at Gershom and he chuckles at me.

Uncle Jon slides a CD into his player and a lady starts singing about being lost and found. I realize that since Uncle Jon was at the same church we were at last night, maybe he could help Gershom and me figure out the difference between being rescued and being saved. Before I can ask, though, Uncle Jon speaks.

"The lady we're going to meet is my wife, your Aunt Karis. The four of us will go to our house first, where you can get cleaned up. After lunch, we'll go visit your mom. How does that sound?"

Gershom whispers, "Thank you." I just nod. I have no words to add.

Aunt Karis is waiting for us in front of a high school, and as we pull up, she raises a paper grocery bag. After getting in the car, she pulls out some clothes and shows us from the front seat. "I know these are probably going to be a little big on you both, but they will do until we can go shopping. Look Jasmine, the shirt I found for you has a 'J' on it, right here by the collar. Isn't that cute? The principal said I could go through the lost and found clothing. I'm sorry you have to make do with someone's discarded clothing."

Uncle Jon lowers his wife's arms. "It's okay, honey. Don't worry. The kids aren't looking to win at fashion week. They'll be fine. Besides, we can go shopping tomorrow."

Aunt Karis turns around and looks at us. "Sorry, kids. I'm just excited. You're probably worn out from that crazy trip you just took, aren't you? A nice warm shower, some leftover cornbread with gravy for lunch, and y'all should be feeling great again in no time."

A shower does sound wonderful. I look at Gershom and he gives me a thumbs up. He leans over and whispers, "Cornbread and gravy sounds a lot better than jelly packets and cold hamburgers, doesn't it?"

I nod, and before we know it, we arrive in front of a beautiful house. The door is painted bright blue, and there is orange trim around each window. A wire wreath hangs on the door in the shape of the letters AU. As we go inside, I point at it, and Aunt Karis explains.

"It stands for Auburn University, where your Uncle Jon teaches. They have a big football team there that we are quite proud of. If you spend any time at all in Alabama, you'll learn real quick that there are two football teams, Auburn and Alabama, that people root for. You'll hear 'War Eagle' and 'Roll Tide' everywhere. It would be best to choose a team and stick with it, and since we like Auburn, I'm gonna suggest you root for them!"

"Karis! The kids have more important things to worry about right now than football." Uncle Jon shakes his head at Aunt Karis.

I think it's funny and pipe up, "It's okay, Uncle Jon. We don't really know much about football, but maybe you can teach us." I wrap my arms around Aunt Karis and look up at her. "I would be happy to be on your team."

Aunt Karis smiles at me and untangles herself from my embrace to point down the hall. "How about you take your shower while I warm up some food?" She hands me my clothes from the paper bag.

I gasp. "Oh, I'm sorry, Aunt Karis. I didn't mean to get your clothes all dirty. I must be so filthy."

Aunt Karis strokes my dry, wild hair. "Not at all, sugar. But I know your brother wants a shower also, so don't take too long, okay?" She smiles at me, and my apprehension disappears.

I feel like a brand-new girl when I sit down at the table to eat. I can barely remember the last time I felt this clean. The gravy is warm and thick, and the cornbread is filling. All those nights sleeping outside on the hard ground have taken their toll, and I almost fall asleep at the table.

Uncle Jon comes over and sits next to me. He takes my hand, causing me to look up. "Would you like to stay here with Aunt Karis this afternoon and take a nap? It might be better if your mother only met one of you at a time anyway. I promise I'll take you to see her tomorrow."

Suddenly, the thought of a soft bed beckons so much more loudly than my elusive mother. I glance at Gershom and he says, "That might be best. We wouldn't want our mother to get overwhelmed, and you do look like you could use a rest."

"Okay," I nod to Uncle Jon. Aunt Karis takes my other hand and leads me down the hallway to their guest room. A huge bed sits in the middle of the room, and Aunt Karis pulls the blanket off. I crawl under the sheet, and she covers me lightly. The pillow is the softest thing I have ever felt, and before I can even mumble "Thank you," I fall blissfully asleep.

23 — Gershom and His Mother

"Here we are," Uncle Jon announced as we pulled into a broad driveway. Huge white gates sat open, allowing us to continue up the drive toward a wide brick building. We drove around the side of the building to park, and when I got out, I inhaled, expecting to smell the abundance of flowers surrounding the place. I coughed several times as the antiseptic smell overpowered the flowers.

"Yeah, they didn't plant fragrant enough flowers to cover up the hospital smell. But this isn't technically a hospital. More like a rehab place, but with permanent residents. You'll see. Come on, they're expecting us." Uncle Jon motioned for me to follow him inside.

I held my breath, unsure of what to expect inside. When I did venture a smell, I was confused. The hospital smell was not as strong in here. It seemed like it should be worse inside.

A nurse came around the desk and greeted us. He stuck his hand out, so I shook it. He told me, "So you're the famous son I've heard about! Jon told me you were coming with him today." We started walking down the hallway, passing many rooms on both sides of the hall. Some doors were open, and some were closed. I wondered if the closed doors were locked from the outside. Was this a rehab place for the crazy?

The nurse continued talking, his voice cadence matching the squeak his shoes made with every other step. "Today is an okay day for Stephanie. She sat at the piano all morning but didn't play anything."

Uncle Jon whispered to me, "Your mother is a great pianist. On her good days, she'll play for hours. On her bad days, she won't even go near the piano."

I nodded my head in understanding. If my mother could play the piano, maybe that explained where my desire to play the saxophone came from. Being in foster care and moving schools so often, there never had been an opportunity to play. However, I had promised myself that as soon as I lived somewhere stable, I would learn how to play, even if that didn't happen until I was an adult.

The nurse led us into a large game room. Uncle Jon thanked him, and we walked through the room onto a back porch.

There, sitting in an overstuffed striped recliner, sat a much older version of Jasmine. I took a step back and shook my head at the similarity.

Uncle Jon patted my back. "It's okay, son."

I gathered my composure and walked up to my mother. "Hello."

She turned her gaze toward me, and while her eyes were the same gray-blue shade that Jasmine's were, hers looked like the sparkle had left quite some time ago.

"Who are you?" Her feeble voice sounded like she was almost a hundred years old.

I looked at Uncle Jon, wondering if I should tell her who I was. He spoke for me. "This is a young boy who would like to get to know you. His name is Gershom."

My mother's eyes widened, and she sat straight up. "I have a son named Gershom. But I lost him. Oh, I lost him so long ago." She started moaning and rocking, and I was afraid we would have to leave.

I reached out and touched my mother's hand. It was soft and warm. "He's not lost anymore. I know where he is. I came to tell you where he is." She stopped rocking, and this time when she looked at me, it was like she peered all the way into my very soul. Jasmine's words came flooding back about me needing someone in my life to touch my soul, and I blinked, trying to stay in the present.

“Are you *my* Gershom? But where is my Jasmine?” My mother raised her hand and rubbed my arm. “If you are here, is my Kasper here, too?”

I knew my dad had died when Jasmine was a baby, and if my mother couldn’t handle being a single parent, she must have convinced herself that she had lost all three of us that day. In her mind, if I were standing here now, then it only made sense that all three of us should be here.

Uncle Jon spoke. “Jasmine will come tomorrow, Stephanie. You can see your daughter tomorrow. Today, Gershom is here.”

For the next several minutes, Uncle Jon talked about nothing in particular while I stared at my mother and she stared back at me. All my hopes and dreams of finally meeting my mother and having a real family slowly ebbed away as the realization sunk in; my mother wasn’t able to be anyone’s parent. How would I break the news to Jasmine?

We only stayed for a short time. The nurse met us on the way out and handed me an envelope. On the front was written “Found in Kasper’s helmet.”

“What’s inside?” I asked.

“Open it and see,” he encouraged.

I peeked inside and pulled out a faded photograph. A toddler in overalls and a baby in a fancy red dress smiled up at me, and I felt an indescribable chill come over me. I was touching a link to my past I never knew existed. The corners were bent, and I looked at the nurse with a question on my face.

"Stephanie asks to hold this picture every day while she waits for her breakfast. When we bring the food, she tells us to keep it safe in its envelope until tomorrow." The nurse turned to my uncle. "Stephanie's psychiatrist wouldn't let us tell you, Jon. I'm terribly sorry! He said it could start a downward spiral and all that, you know. But I figure, since Gershom is here now…" his voice trailed off.

Uncle Jon's cheek twitched. I recognized that same sign of anger when I let my frustration build for too long.

I handed the picture back to the nurse. I wanted so badly to ask if I could keep it, but I knew my mother expected to hold it tomorrow morning, and I didn't want to take that small comfort from her.

On the way back to the Greene's house, I waited until Uncle Jon's fingers relaxed around the steering wheel before asking about everything Paul and Jasmine and even that strange preacher in North Carolina had said about God.

"It's not so much the words you use, but the attitude you have that makes the difference," Uncle Jon explained. "In the very beginning, when God made the first people—Adam and Eve—He made them to be His friends. Adam, Eve, and God would walk and talk and generally just have a good time together. But then Adam and Eve did something wrong—they sinned—and God can't have sin in Heaven. So, He sent His Son Jesus to take our sin away, so that when we die, we can go to Heaven. Following me so far?"

I nodded. "Makes sense. If God can't have sin in Heaven, we could only get there if we didn't have sin, either."

"That's right," Uncle Jon nodded. "A lot of people think they can get to Heaven on their own, by being a good person or doing good things. But only trusting Jesus to take our sin away can get us to Heaven. The amazing thing is all you have to do is ask! If you know that you have sin, and you can't make it to Heaven on your own, just ask Jesus to forgive your sin."

"That does sound pretty easy." Easier than I thought it would be. I had thought surely Jasmine must have misunderstood Paul or something, but she was definitely old enough to understand this and go to Heaven.

"God made it that way on purpose, so that even little children can understand and go to Heaven."

I smiled when Uncle Jon voiced what I had thought. "Thank you for explaining it. I should think about it and figure out what I need to do." I opened my door and went inside. The day had been a roller coaster for my mind, first with my mother and now with this. I went into the guest room to take my own nap.

Jasmine was just getting up, and after promising to tell her all about it at supper, I crashed onto the bed and fell fast asleep.

24 — Gershom's Adoption

I tiptoed down the hallway. The digital clock on the bedside table had read 12:17 when I woke up. I figured my mid-afternoon nap had messed up my circadian rhythm—something Jasmine talked about all the time, how sleeping at strange times will make sleeping at night harder, or something—and I thought maybe a cup of warm milk would help me get back to sleep. The kitchen light was on, and when I got closer to the doorway, I heard my aunt and uncle talking softly.

"So tomorrow first thing in the morning, I'm going to call New York social services." Uncle Jon's voice was quiet, and I strained to hear. "I know Kasper was originally from Binghamton, so I'll call that city first. I don't know why, but I feel like

Stephanie would have at least taken the kids back there to leave them."

I peeked around the corner and saw Aunt Karis place her hand on Uncle Jon's arm. She whispered back a reply, and Uncle Jon nodded. He continued, "Maybe these kids are the answer to our prayers about expanding our family. We knew we couldn't have a baby for a reason. Maybe God wants us to raise my sister's kids."

"Oh, Jon!" Aunt Karis squealed. "We can't send them back to New York!"

"Shh! You'll wake the kids!" Uncle Jon whispered.

I stepped into the kitchen. "It's all right, I'm already awake. Are you going to send us back? Please let Jasmine meet our mother first, at least." A lump formed in my throat at the thought of going back to New York, but I knew I needed to keep a brave face in front of my aunt and uncle.

Aunt Karis motioned for me to sit down next to her. "We don't want to send you back. In fact, we were talking about keeping you both here, with us. What do you think of that?"

I looked at Uncle Jon. He smiled at me and raised his eyebrows. "You mean, you want us to stay with you—like kinship care?" My entire life, I had wanted real parents, and during this trip I had hoped that my mother would be my mother again. When I saw what a sorry mess she was this afternoon, I had adjusted my expectations and was preparing myself to live out the rest of my days in foster care. Why had I never thought about kinship care?

"Um," Uncle Jon glanced at Aunt Karis. "What is kinship care?"

"Oh, it's like foster care, but it's a relative instead of a stranger taking care of the kid," I explained.

"I see." Aunt Karis nodded at Uncle Jon. He told me, "Then not like kinship care."

My world quaked once again. My mother couldn't handle me, and now my aunt and uncle didn't want me either. The thought occurred to me that if no one on earth wanted me, why would God want me?

"We want you to stay here as our own kids. We want to adopt you into our family."

My eyes flew up to Uncle Jon. "Wha—" Adopt? We were too old to be adopted, and we knew it. Not since the fiasco at the Peterson's had we thought about adoption.

Aunt Karis took my hand, and Uncle Jon laughed a little. "You should see the look on your face! You look like you just won the lottery, but you hadn't bought any tickets."

I nodded. That was kind of what it felt like. I knew I shouldn't be at all excited, but the emotions of the past few days threatened to overwhelm me. "I should think about this." I got up and trailed down the hallway in a daze. These people really did want me. I knew others had said that before, but there was something different in Jon and Karis's eyes. Maybe God really wanted me, too.

When I got to the bedroom, Jasmine was sitting up. "What's all that noise?" she asked sleepily.

I sat on the edge of the bed, and as I spoke, I could hear the wonder in my voice. "Jaz, they want to adopt us."

"Really?" Jasmine sucked in all the air she could fit into her lungs. "Can they?" she squeaked.

I shrugged my shoulders. "I don't see why not. It would start out as kinship care, then the paperwork should go through without a problem, seeing as how our mother is in that facility and will never be able to take care of us properly." I heard a tinge of bitterness creep into my voice, but Jasmine didn't seem to notice.

She stood up on the bed and gave a huge bounce. "Yippee!" she yelled.

Light from the hallway suddenly spilled onto the bed and hit Jasmine's legs. We both climbed off the bed and stepped over to our new parents-to-be. Jasmine tipped her head up at Aunt Karis and grinned. "Can I give you a hug now? I'm all clean still."

Aunt Karis bent down and wrapped Jasmine in both arms. "Clean or dirty, I'll never refuse a hug from my precious girl."

Uncle Jon clapped his hand on my back. "Kids, we can't do anything about it tonight. The best thing would be to go back to sleep, and we'll make all the arrangements tomorrow morning, okay?"

We leaped back in bed and said good night. The adults turned off the light and closed our door. I turned to Jasmine, and we held hands.

"Will I still get to visit Mother tomorrow?" she whispered.

"Yeah, I think we'll both get to visit her a lot, now that we'll live here."

"You know, I'm glad it worked out this way instead. Now we'll have a mom *and* a dad, and by adopting us, we know that they *chose* us. It's just like what God does when we ask Him into our heart. He *chooses* us, Gersh. All we have to do is ask. And the good thing about God is that it doesn't take months of red tape."

Jasmine's passionate speech gave me another lump in my throat. As she rolled over to go to sleep, I was glad it was dark, because tears squeezed out of my eyes. There was no question in my mind about God now. I knew He was real. I knew He loved me and had been watching out for me my whole life. And more than ever, I knew I needed Him in my heart. I sniffed and sat up on one elbow.

Whether or not the adoption with Uncle Jon and Aunt Karis would go through, I was going to be adopted into God's family tonight, and I knew that this was one adoption that could never be overturned. I closed my eyes, and in three minutes, God had done something I never dreamed was possible—He finalized my first adoption. I came down here in search of a forever family, but suddenly, I knew why God led me to Alabama—and finding my birth mother was only part of it.

I rolled onto my back, listening to Jasmine's even breathing in the quiet night. My eyes closed, peace filling my heart, and I slipped back to sleep, excited to see what my future might hold.

Bible verses for why we are sinners and how to be saved:

1. Admit you are a sinner. God is perfect and cannot let any sin into Heaven, and every person has been a sinner since birth.
   --Romans 3:23 - For all have sinned, and come short of the glory of God.
   --Romans 5:12 - Wherefore, as by one man sin entered into the world, and death by sin; and so death passed upon all men, for that all have sinned.
2. Believe that Jesus Christ died for your sin and rose from the dead to live again in Heaven. Because no sin is allowed in Heaven, God's Son came to Earth to take our punishment for sin. He shed His blood to make a way for us to join God in Heaven.
   --Romans 5:8 - But God commendeth his love toward us, in that, while we were yet sinners, Christ died for us.
   --Romans 6:23 - For the wages of sin *is* death; but the gift of God *is* eternal life through Jesus Christ our Lord.
   --1 Thessalonians 4:14 - For if we believe that Jesus died and rose again, even so them also which sleep in Jesus will God bring with him.
3. Confess Him as Lord. Jesus took our punishment. All we have to do is accept His free gift--and when God looks at us, He will only see Jesus' blood, thereby allowing us into Heaven.

--Romans 10:9-10 - That if thou shalt confess with thy mouth the Lord Jesus, and shalt believe in thine heart that God hath raised him from the dead, thou shalt be saved.

--Romans 10:13 - For whosoever shall call upon the name of the Lord shall be saved.

4. Delight in the fact that you are now on your way to Heaven. If you are trusting in God alone (Jesus' sacrifice and nothing more) to cleanse your sin and get you to Heaven, there is nothing that can change your eternal destination.

   --John 10:28-29 - And I give unto them eternal life; and they shall never perish, neither shall any *man* pluck them out of my hand. My Father, which gave *them* me, is greater than all; and no *man* is able to pluck *them* out of my Father's hand.

   --Romans 8:38-39 - For I am persuaded, that neither death, nor life, nor angels, nor principalities, nor powers, nor things present, nor things to come, nor height, nor depth, nor any other creature, shall be able to separate us from the love of God, which is in Christ Jesus our Lord.

   --1 John 1:9 - If we confess our sins, he is faithful and just to forgive us *our* sins, and to cleanse us from all unrighteousness.

Acknowledgements

Thanks to Nanowrimo for inspiring me to write a novel in one month, even though it took me four more years to get this book published, and another three to get it edited and republished.

Thanks to my awesome beta readers: Johanna, Tascha, and Becky. Without your encouragement and advice, this book would not be half as good as it is. Thanks also to my sensitivity readers: Mia, Alisa, and all the authors from The Writing Gals Critique Group on Facebook. You were all so helpful! Mary, no one more so than you.

Thanks to my friends and family along the entire East Coast, who helped me with region-specific research. Several adventures the siblings have are based on real events.

Thanks to my friends at Heritage Baptist Church for allowing me to add you into this story.

Thanks to my amazing cover designer, Heather Wilson, for your beautiful rendition of the kids. I can't wait to see what you come up with for book two!

Made in the USA
Middletown, DE
11 May 2022

65637935R00090